FACES OF DEATH

RESURRECTION

MONTY

authorHOUSE®

AuthorHouse™
1663 Liberty Drive
Bloomington, IN 47403
www.authorhouse.com
Phone: 833-262-8899

Published by AuthorHouse 04/01/2022

ISBN: 978-1-6655-5640-8 (sc)
ISBN: 978-1-6655-5639-2 (e)

Library of Congress Control Number: 2022906113

Contents

The Breakdown

It seems as if things change doing the time when the discovery was made behind the Faces of Death murders case. Of how the lives of Jill, Jason & Christian would soon turn out. Considering how they manage to uncover the mystery behind the ruthless Halloween murders. That instill fear throughout this country's history. That their story was made famous by the media who display it to the world. Making the three of them famous for revealing the truth behind the mystery? Even though, there were some help in that department from someone. Who wanted to remain anonymous? Which is something Jill & her two buddies couldn't bring themselves to understand? Of why this person didn't come forward? Considering that all is now at its wit's end of finally closing that chapter of your life for good? However, there still were a bit of concern on the matter. Of what was mentioned in a text message from this anonymous person. Who happened to mention that" This is where things get interesting"? Which arouse their curiosity on what exactly does that means? As the jury is still out on that one? However, it is something Lisa didn't want to look over. As it is her sworn duty to get to the bottom of each nook & cranny that must deal with this case. In the meanwhile, things begin to look up for the three of them. As Jill decided to stay with Jason for a little while to assist his injury while he recovers. From his gunshot wound he receive while protecting her from the killer. Which took place at the House of Horrors haunted house. While at the same time using their fame to bring awareness to pay tribute to all the lives that has been lost doing those murders. To have a fundraiser for the victim's family. Doing their time of grief?

Christian, however, was a sensational writer, who made headlines. With his journal creativity of wanting to write a book on his experience. Of what it was like doing those dark times with the killers. Which is a project? He & Lisa is currently working on together. The three of them couldn't imagine the type of popularity they receive from the public. As the interviews begin to row in with top executive anchors from top rated news broadcast stations. As people wanted to know what it was like to be a victim in those horrific murders. Words alone doesn't even begin to describe the horror that they had to face. Which was mentioned in several interviews by the three of them. That once the book comes out. The people would then have somewhat of a better understanding about what the three of them had to go through? However, there was one thing Jill & Jason wanted to know about Christian. That had to deal with the house of horrors. That had to deal with him knowing what he knew about the two killers. When he was held captive by the killers inside of the haunted maze. Since they wanted to know how he escaped. Also, the fact that how did he know they were in trouble. Christian simply explains. That he was knock unconscious by the killer. Then regain conscious once he heard someone talking on the walkie talkie near him. Which so happens to be Danny Burton explaining to them both about what took place. However, while regaining conscious he could see someone walking away in a monk robe. Only to find out that his restraints had been removed by this mystery person. Which got Jill & Jason thinking about the witness Danny Burton & Edgerrin James was referring too? That whoever this person is? Wanted to remain anonymous for some apparent reason? However, the three of them couldn't help but, to feel as if there is more to this story that meets the eye.

Considering how they were left with the question of what lies ahead of them. Of what this person's intentions are? When left in the dark about a message that seem too conspicuous. That had them thinking seriously about finding out who this person is? Which is sort of hard to do when there is nothing to go on with? That whoever this person is? Seem like a ghost in their eyes. Being interview by the press also help with the search for Elizabeth Burton remains. Which was recover by the police two days after the interview. Meanwhile, a upcoming film studio was in talk of making a documentary film on a family based on an urban legend tale. Who was seriously considering Jill, Jason & Christian as stars in their movie? Which would give off good rates if the three of them decides to star in this film. Which would be directed by a young producer who go by the name of Zorn the Magnificent? Due to his magnificent film present of capturing the highlights of movie magic. Which is how he gotten his name sort of speak? The film is based on a family that went on a killing spree together. Killing dozens of people throughout their history? That have some people saying that it is one of the most notorious events to ever take place. That according to legend the bodies of the victims still remain in the mansion. Where they lie dormant with the killer's family. Which was known as the" Carson Family"? Who called their mansion the Carson's Tower? Where they would open their doors to total strangers to stay the night in their lovely mansion. Which was sort like staying in a hotel? Which is where they get you! According to the tale? That whoever steps inside the mansion, doesn't make it out alive & never heard from again? That based on the urban legend tale. The spirits of the deceased still haunt the premises of the Carson's Tower. Especially, the Carson Family who still seeks out the people who dares enter their domain.

Which is a great opportunity for an upcoming producer to showcase his talents. By directing his first film on his own for the first time. However, his hardest test yet is trying to convince Jill & her two comrades to feature in his film. Which proves to be challenging. Considering that the three of them are busy these days with different appointments. That if somehow, he can squeeze in a little of their time. Hoping that he can negotiate some sort of deal with the three of them. So, Zorn decided to contact them personally over the phone. To see if he can schedule an appointment with the three of them. They all agree to meet with him the following week. As Zorn assistant Laura made the appointment for the upcoming week. However, Jill felt it was unnecessary to meet with this person. Considering that it is too soon for this sort of thing. As Christian & Jason told her to just relax. That this sort of opportunity doesn't come very often? That this is an opportunity of a lifetime to finally feel normal again? An experience of what it's like to show the lighter side of them. Instead of always being stuck on the dark side of things that happened in the past. Jill still wasn't sold on the idea of doing this sort of thing. However, she did agree to go along with them to see what this film is all about? The day finally came to meet with Mr. Zorn on the film. He begins by telling them about the history behind the Carson's Tower. Also, what they plan to do with the production? As it was made clear to the three of them that it is just a documentary & that no harm would come to them. That the goal is for the three of them to star in this documentary, so that his film can make headlines. Since it sort of relates to their own story. Which would also boost up the sale on their book when it is release.

Which sort of make sense to the three of them about financing their book. By starring in a film like their life story. In which, both parties can benefit from?

Not to mention the amount of money they would receive for doing this. Which is a win sort of deal for the three of them. Christian thought that maybe he can create some revenue by writing a column in the paper about the upcoming event. Being a journalist & all, he could bring attention to this film. Which would create even more hype for the film when it is release. It seems as if both parties were in an agreement about how they can help each other benefit from this little ordeal. Zorn told the three of them that the film will be in production this summer. In the meanwhile, the search was on to find a few actors who can star alongside Jill, Jason & Christian. He seems to have found six upcoming actors to star in his film. Four guys & two girls who go by the names of Jade Summers, Alex Crawford, Layla Martinez, Jake Martin, Elliot Smith & Seth Myers. Zorn even hired his longtime friend Timothy Jones to run the technical support for the film. Considering that he would oversee the use of the equipment. Meanwhile, Christian broke the good news to Lisa about starring in a film. That they would have to put their book on hold for a little while. Lisa was very supportive of Christian. However, she wasn't about to put their book on hold until he finishes the film. She told him that maybe they can work in between takes. Only if she can stroll along with him on set to work alongside him on the book. Since they have a time frame for when the book is release. As usual, it seems as if Lisa manages to talk her way into persuading Christian to let her go with him on set to finish their book. Even though, things seem a bit relax for Jill, Christian & Jason. The truth of the matter was that social media wasn't very kind to the three of them. Due to some comments that was made by certain individuals who just didn't have anything else to do. Except for being critical to others with their smart remarks.

Usually, they don't even bother reading some of the comments. However, there was one who just got under their skin. Who go under the name Eric Johnson for some apparent reason? Being that he was misunderstood by many which he pays for in blood. By the many that accused him of murder that had many people disgusted with the system. As this person just went in on Jill for what she did to him. Which is the one thing that is still eating away at her. Which is a constant reminder to her everyday by this person's comments toward her. Sending her some very nasty comments to her twitter page. Jason told her not to pay it no mind. Because they have no idea what all she has been through?

However, one night Jill was up late on the computer. As she receives an e-mail from no one other than the so call protester for Eric Johnson. At first, Jill wasn't going to read it, but she was curious to see what this person has to say? What she read was something out of the ordinary? She didn't know whether it was a threat or a warning. The e-mail read" Beware the Bucket list, in result to the fear of death"? Which was something Jill couldn't wrap her finger around. So, she shows Jason the e-mail the very next day. He too couldn't figure it out. As he told Jill to forget about it & pay it no mind? That it is just someone trying to get under her skin. That all this person wants is publicity. Jill took Jason's advice to ignore this person completely. The three of them continue with life as they know it. As the production for the documentary was underway to start filming in a couple of weeks. As the three of them along with Lisa went to the studio to go over some details about what exactly is expected of them. Also, to meet the other cast & crew who will be working on this project along with them. The six actors were in shock to find out that they will be working with certified pros who have live through this sort of thing. Which made Jill, Christian & Jason even more excited to do this film. Do to the fact that these young actors lookup to the three of them including Lisa for that matter.

CHAPTER 2

Carson's Tower

With everything they have going over with the routine to begin filming the first scene. By documenting everyone opinion on the Carson's Tower. Capturing the insight from the cast by getting them to introduce themselves. Everyone seems nerves at first, but as they moved along. One by one they started to get use of the camera in their face. Zorn seem delighted to headline the story in his own words. Before they all head up to the mansion to start filming up there. When they finish filming the first scene of the movie. They all hop into different vehicle & drove off into the sunset. Everyone seems excited at this point of what they can expect when they reach the mansion. However, before reaching their destination? Zorn decided to stop along the way to talk to a couple of locals in the area. To see if they could give him some info on the mansion, while the cameraman films them. Some cooperated while others didn't want to have anything to do with it. However, they manage to run into one individual who witness the horrors inside of the mansion. Who somehow survive one night in the tower & live to talk about it? His name was Todd Williams. It seems as if the poor man was talking out of his head not making any sense, whatsoever? As the things he describes that went on in there, just didn't make sense. As Todd try to warn them not to go up there under no circumstances? Which seem all too real to Jill, Jason & Christian who was reminded of the horrors they went through. Lisa however, thought that the man was craze & delusional? Which they all thought in their minds. Considering that there is no such thing as ghost going around killing people. Which seems absurd as they all shook their heads at the man, while grinning?

After they manage to get some footage of the locals, they pack up everything

*& headed out to the mansion. As they were on their way up to the mansion.
Elliot spotted a couple of witchcraft symbols made from tree branches. That
was hanging from some trees in the woods near the mansion. Which could
be a warning sign that they are getting closer to the mansion. Which was all
caught on data as Jade stop to give a brief statement behind these symbols.
Since she studies witchcraft as a profession. It seems as if these different images
symbolize death itself. Which results in a deadly game called Mindhunter's? A
game that must deal with a person psyche of mentoring the fear of death. Which
was a light that went off in Jill & Jason's head. Of having to remember that
statement in the e-mail sent by someone using Eric's name. How unusual the
two of them thought to themselves. Knowing that the fear of death is a symbol
for the Faces of Death curse. Which seem very odd & strange of what it means.
Which got the two of them thinking about the text message that said," This is
where things get interesting"? Another link in the chain that has been missing.
Of how it got them thinking that maybe they should follow the signs. Which
will eventually lead to this anonymous person they have been searching for?
They then ran the news by Christian & Lisa who realize what was going on.
The fact that them being here is no coincidence? That maybe someone in this
film is the missing link. Lisa had suggested that maybe they should interact
with each of cast member to see what happens next? That some where's lies a
secret within this film. Which was why maybe the three of them was chosen to
do this movie. However, they didn't want to alarm anyone. So, they decided
to play it by ear. However, once they were done shooting the footage of the
witchcraft symbols. They all head up to the mansion to start the filming there.*

*Once they reach their destination it seems as if suddenly a weird feeling came
over everyone. Of how eerie this place really is? Which gave off an unpleasant
vibe of creepiness. Of how the mansion seems as if it's been abandoned for
decades on in. Which is surrounded by a wooded area that have lots of crows
flying around the mansion. Not to mention, the fact that the mansion almost
resembles a tower. Which is why it was called the Carson's Tower? Which Zorn
explain on camera as they begin filming the mansion. The crew begin moving
the equipment from the truck into the front gate of the mansion. Do to the
fact that they had to park outside the gate because of the large solid wall that
surrounds the property. Seth begins teasing the crew by making spooky sounds.
As they begin to head for the front door. It seems as if Zorn ran into a little
luck. By locating the key that was under the mat. He then unlocks the door &*

started to head in, when suddenly! Out came a flock of bats that scare everyone as they ran away. Talking about a close call? They all laugh nervously at one another. As they were heading inside of the house Alex & Seth begin whistling the theme song from Tales from the dark side. To try & scare Jade & Layla as the two of them enter the mansion. Before exploring the mansion Zorn told everyone to stay together. Because of this place history of having all sorts of bobby traps that is located throughout the mansion. The inside of this place seems very haunted like? The fact that they all got some very bad vibes from just standing in the hallway. As Laura, Zorn's assistant thought that this is a very bad place & that they should take Todd advice to not stay. Jake however, thought that this could be the opportunity of a lifetime to break into the business. As of being notice by top executive in the film industry to take interest in their project. Which is something they all can agree on by making this film?

So, without any further ado, Zorn & his team begin filming the raw footage about the Carson's Family home. While the crew set up the equipment to catch anything unusual on the camera. While in the process of setting up the equipment some of the crew members recalled hearing some very unusual sounds throughout the mansion. When they all got set up & ready to begin documenting the different parts of the mansion. Fear grew substantially sufficient as the cast & crew slowly walk throughout the mansion. While Zorn gives a bit of history on what part of the mansion was relevant. Meanwhile, Jade was trying to get in contact with the spirits of the Carson's family. A family of six who killed their guest in a ruthless manner. By playing games with the guest who stayed in their lovely mansion. Sort of a crazy family who seem unpredictable at times. However, their names were starting with the father was Ben Carson. Follow by the mother Ella Carson & their four children. Who names were Sam Carson, Rachel Carson, Tom Carson & Diane Carson. Who all wore scary costumes to scare their victim's? It was sort of like their costumes was self-made as a reflection to resemble who they were as a family. Which was a couple of hillbillies who moved into the mansion. There were all sorts of evidence surrounding this place. Of the killing that took place inside the mansion. One being the dry up blood handprints of people's hands that stain the walls throughout the mansion. While another showed witchcraft symbols written on other parts of the wall. The same ones that were in the woods on their way up to the mansion. Which was getting a little too intense for Jill, Jason, Christian & Lisa. Who seem a bit baffle about this story that has been laid upon them? Which seems a little close to home. Considering that it is starting to remind them of their story. Which to them seem like another clue in the case by getting them closer to the truth.

They all stayed together on venturing the mansion while filming its history. Until that is? When two of the cast members went missing from the group. That being Jake Martin & Layla Martinez who just vanish into thin air. Zorn & the others try to locate them through the walkie talkie. To see if they have fallen into one of the hidden compartments, he had warned them about? Considering that this mansion has many? At first, they begin to pick up static from the walkie talkie, but that would soon change. When they begin to hear voices of the dead on the walkie talkies. Follow by static, which was hard for them to make out what was being said? Then from out of no where's came this horrifying moan. That scare the living daylight's out of everyone. As they all started to look at each other with a concern expression. As the voices on the other end of the walkie talkie begin calling out each person's name. Which put them in an awkward position, as the voices begin to get louder. However, nothing would prepare them for what would happen next? When one of the doors down the hall slam shut. Causing everyone to jump in fear even though everyone at that point was willing to leave. Including Jill, Jason, Lisa & Christian who took off running. Behind Jade & Elliot who didn't waste no time at all? Meanwhile, Zorn, Alex & Seth try to catch up with them. So that they don't get separate from one another with the crew members not far behind. Filming every inch of the event. While running, they could hear Layla & Jake laughing on the walkie talkie. Which now cause everyone to stop running in disbelief? The fact that it takes two individuals to ruin it for everyone. As the two of them appear down the hall laughing hysterically at what they did? Which didn't appear to be all that funny to the others. Even though, they understood the reality of the joke which was humoring to say the least. Which was all part of the documentary to show the humor side of this film. Which was all stage to scare Jill & her friends in hope that it will make the film even scarier.

CHAPTER 3

The Tower's Mystery

It seems as if Jake & Layla couldn't help themselves as the opportunity presented itself. As the temptation was too great not to seize the moment. Which was a huge lift off everyone's shoulders of not being too tense. Considering that after all it's just a documentary & nothing more? As the sun begin to set in the night sky. Zorn decided to call it a day considering that the mansion was a huge residence & couldn't be film in one day. Not to mention, that the tower seems a bit terrifying at night. Which would be an easy way to get lost in the dark, so they all headed back down to the living room. Where they had everything setup. It was at that moment when Lisa saw her opportunity to chat with the cast to see if she can dig up some information. On each one of them to see where they stand in this case. By investigating them. She found out some very interesting things in the process. Like how, Jade loves to take on the persona of others by studying them. Which tells the story of how she can describe a person's intellect. By just looking at them that helps her with her psychic ability skills. Which sort of speech for itself? While Elliot loves to play the part of the mysterious one. Who is very carefully guarded about letting certain people in on his life? However, he seems like a very down to earth person. Who seem very interested in being part of this film? Alex on the other hand seem a bit relax about the whole thing. As Lisa took him to be sort of a thinker? In which she could tell just by talking to him. Seth, however, was the life of the party sort of speech. Who seem delighted to be in the presents of Jill, Jason & Christian for some apparent reason? Meanwhile, the other two, Jake & Layla the two pranksters seem a bit outgoing.

To the point that has Lisa concern about what are they planning next?

Almost as if the two of them are planning something big? Which is the vibe she is getting from speaking to the two of them. Lisa explains to Jill, Jason & Christian that there is some shady characters amongst this group of people. That being the cast of the film. Not to mention, the crew members that she has yet to investigate. Along with the director Zorn the Magnificent who may have a few issues she has yet to explore. Which seems like they step into uncharted territory at this point. Of not being able to connect the dots to reveal the truth behind the matter. Of what's the real purpose behind this film. That the purpose is to reveal some hidden message. According to Jill & her friends who are looking for some sort of sign that reveals who this anonymous person is? Who knows of the Faces of Death murders? That their suspicion lies within this film that seem so close to home for the four of them. Later, that night after supper? Jill receives a phone call from her mother who decided to check in on her. Since her close call with death at the House of Horrors. Which created a closer relationship between mother & daughter since that unfaithful night. They chatted for quite a bit before calling it a night. However, before hanging up? Jill's mother told her about a letter she receives in the mail for her. Jill then asks, her mother who was it from? As her mother had no idea who sent the letter. So, Jill told her mother to open it up & read it to her. Which read" Beware the signs of the bucket list, in result to the fear of death"? Which had them both puzzle on what exactly does that means? As Jill try to make sense of it? Considering that she is dumbfounded by the letter of what bucket list she must beware of? Which didn't make no sense to her at all of what that means. Even though, she had a good feeling on who may have sent it? Which is the same individual who sent those nasty remarks to her twitter page.

Who go under the name Eric Johnson who has been constantly harassing her? As she tries to put two & two together with the messages she has receive from this person. Who is also someone who is anonymous? Which seems all too familiar to her. Which got her thinking about the message that said," This is where things get interesting"? Which seems like what is now going on? Which didn't make no sense whatsoever? Of how this person help them reveal who the killers were & then deliver a message so complex. That it doesn't resonate visually. So, Jill decided from this moment on to keep her eyes open for anything unusual that has to deal with signs. Which got her thinking about what Lisa said' about the cast of this film. In the meanwhile, everyone gathers around to talk about the mansion so far. Given everyone's definition about the film &

what it means to be part of this project. They all seem grateful to be a part of something great. Which led to the discussion about the Faces of Death murders case. In which, Jill & her friends begin to explain the difficulties they had to endure doing that time. Which instantly turn sour as the jokes begin to pour in by the cast & crew on what they would do if they were in their shoes. There were some individuals who seem delighted by Jill & her friends' story. While others thought that it was no laughing matter. Which got Jill curious about certain aspect of the behavior of some individuals who seem to take interest in their story. However, just as things were beginning to become clear to Jill & her friends. They all begin to experience the mansion for what it is. Which is a mansion that is haunted by the spirits of the dead. As they all witness the tower come to life, as the doors in the mansion begin to slam shut. Which was sort of strange considering that there was no video of the doors being slam shut on the surveillance camera. Which was setup throughout parts of the mansion. Which kind of spook everyone at that point? On whether the legend is real about the Carson's Tower?

To some, it all seems like a bunch of hocus pocus nonsense that it is someone in the group trying to scare them. The only problem was that no one would own up to it? Zorn told everyone that at night the tower comes to life. Which got some of them thinking that it was him who might have pull a couple of strings. In order to fool everyone into believing that the mansion is haunted. Which would make his film much darker & scarier. Which didn't fool anyone for that matter of what he wouldn't do to create movie magic. Which is how he gotten his name according to Lisa & the others. Zorn swore it wasn't him that is doing this, but everyone in the room seems convince it was? At that point, the doors would stop shutting throughout the mansion. The cast & crew all seem restless at this point & decided to call it a night. Later on, that night while everyone else was asleep. Christian & Lisa was up working on their book together. While working on the book, Lisa seems distracted for some apparent reason. Almost as if something was troubling her. Which Christian pickup on, considering that her mind was some place other than the book. He then asks her what was wrong. "Lisa told him "That something about this whole thing just feels wrong. Christian couldn't agree more. As he had that same feeling. That for some reason? It seems as if they are being played. Almost as if the four of them are being mock in the sense of all of this? That there is something about this documentary that doesn't set right with him. "Lisa agree" & said, that something is up with this group of people. That judging from the conversation she had with the cast. It seems as if something was up? Especially, with the director who seem very skeptical about why he wanted them to do this film. That he is willing to do anything to create movie magic. Which is something they must watch out for, considering that he has already played his hand.

The two would stay up chatting for a little while longer before finally falling asleep. The next day Jill & Jason woke up to someone screaming in the room. Which got everyone's attention as well? As it turns out that it was Jade Summers who was screaming & yelling? Jill & the others realize that the screaming was coming from the surveillance room. Which was located down the hall in the dayroom. At that point, everyone quicky got up & rush down to the dayroom. To see what was going on. When they got to the room, they seen that Jade & Timothy was at the table going over the surveillance video from last night. Jade call everyone over to look at what happen last night while they all were sleeping. One of the camera's shows proofs that the spirits of the Carson's family does exist. As the video show an image of one of the doors in the mansion opening up & closing by itself. Which was the room Layla was in at that present time. When suddenly! The image of Ben Carson appears momentarily on camera standing on the end of the bed Layla was in. Wearing one of the most bizarre costumes ever made. Which was originally made by him personally to strike fear in a person. Ben then looks up at the camera when suddenly it went blank. Words alone doesn't begin to describe the type of fear that came over everyone at that moment. As they all rush up to the room to see what had happen to Layla. As it turns out that Layla was no where's to be found. Which got everyone thinking where could she be? Then suddenly? The thought came to some of them that maybe she is trying to seek attention once again, by doing this. That once more she & Jake are up to their normal routine. Which brings up the question where was Jake by the way? As he too was missing in action this morning as well.

CHAPTER 4

Strange Things

The search was on to try & find Jake as they call out his name constantly throughout the mansion. Come to find out that he was outside the mansion. Sitting on the porch watching the sun rise. Jake seems confused as of why everyone seems so out of it this morning. As Alex ask him" Does he even know what is going on. Jake then shook his head & said no? Which answer that question that he doesn't have the slightest clue about what is going on? So, they broke the story to him about Layla situation. At first, he thought that they were pulling his leg, but when he seen how serious they were. He demanded to see the video for himself. No matter how hard Jake try to convince the other that it wasn't him? He couldn't help but to laugh as he couldn't keep a straight face. Which cause everyone in the room to put their hands on their heads. In relief that it was only a joke? Jake then admitted that the whole thing was stage to scare everyone. Which was all caught on camera as part of the documentary. Which was genius? On the part of Zorn who plan the whole scene. That the expression on their faces was priceless. Which was worth it in the end. Jake reveals to everyone that Layla was, okay? That she is hiding in the cellar beneath the mansion. They all went down to the cellar to get Layla because now it was time to eat. However, when Jake calls out to Layla to come out from hiding. She didn't appear to oblige to his response. Which seem kind of weird that she didn't answer or come out from hiding. Which to the others seem like another scam to get them to fall for another one of their tricks? Which Jake promises that it wasn't? Which made him concern over the matter. As he begins to yell out in a concern voice into the dark cellar for Layla. Which had everyone taking part in the game by also calling out for Layla. As they joke around constantly while Jake was serious at this point. Seth on the other hand try to get Jake to lighten up a bit.

As he tries to explain to Jake that Layla is trying to pull a fast one on them by trying to take the game one step further. In which, Jake caught on too, as well & decided to play along with the others. So, they decided to play along with Layla by going down into the cellar to look for her. Thinking to themselves that she is willing to play a game of hide & seek. As it turns out that neither of them had no luck with finding her. However, the joke was on Jill, Jason & Christian? As it suddenly became a no laughing matter when Lisa found the mask of fear. One of the three Faces of Death masks. That was located near some pictures of the three of them on the wall. Which has gone a little too far? For Jill & her friends. As they demanded to know what the meaning is for this. Everyone at that moment seem lost for words as of what to make of this misunderstanding. That the only person they can think of? That may have done this was no one other than Layla. Who was the only one down there last night? Which is kind of strange considering that no one could find her. This made Jill upset as she storms up the steps. Which cause Jason to flip out considering that they would stoop this far. For a little entertainment at their expense. Which infuriated Christian & Lisa as they went to calm Jason down. Who went to see about Jill? Zorn went up to apologize to the four of them about the incident. That he is sorry for the actions of his team for finding humor in every little thing. That he is going to fire the person responsible for this. Which is Layla? That this time Layla has gone too far? Zorn then? Gave them his word, that once she shows up. He was going to deal with her personally. In which, he promises to not let happened again? If they decide to stay & finish the film. Jill & the others decided to stay & finish the film since his apology was sincere. However, Jill had a few words of her own. She wanted to express personally to Layla once she sees her again.

As time went on, there still was no sign of Layla any where's to be found. Which got Zorn thinking that maybe she has venture through other parts of the mansion on her own. That maybe, she slips through one of the hidden compartments in the tower. Which could be devastated if she falls into the wrong one. Considering that the mansion is huge & that a person could get lost if not careful. So, Zorn & the crew decided to go & look for her, along with Jill & her friends. Zorn told everyone to stick together & not venture off on their own. Since the tower has many surprises. The camera crew also tag along to capture the whole thing on film. While searching the mansion for Layla. Jill decided to speak with Zorn to thank him for being understanding about their situation. Zorn told her that he understands their issue with the Faces of Death masks & that it shouldn't have been taken out of contact by anyone. Jill then asks, Zorn was that his real name. He told her that his real name was Zack Crenshaw. That Zorn was his stage name in the film industry. Jill also happens to mention the slamming of the doors last night. As she wanted to know was it his doing? He then smile & added he didn't know what she was referring too? As they both started to laugh? They then came to the part of the mansion where the surveillance cameras weren't set up. Which is the part of the mansion they have never venture through. They all begin to call out to Layla to see if she maybe trap in one of the hidden compartments in the tower. In which, they don't have a clue on where these hidden compartments are located throughout the mansion. As it turns out that they weren't getting no response back from her. Which seems weird that a person can just disappear into thin air. Without any traces of where they have gone. In which, many can argue the case that the story of this mansion is true. That whoever steps inside, isn't heard from again?

Which could be the case with Layla as she is now a part of this mansion. Which made the fear of this place even greater than before? As Jade started to have that feeling in her gut that something was wrong. That now is the time to get out while they still can, before it is too late. At that point, the others had decided they wanted to leave. Including Jill & her friends as they decided that play time was over. However, it seems as though, Zorn was responsible for everyone. He told everyone that they weren't going to leave without Layla. That she just maybe some where's in the mansion. That if they wait, she will turn up. Which started an argument between Seth Myers & Zorn? Who argue constantly over what the best thing they should do, at this point? Which wasn't getting them any where's by arguing over the matter. They then came to an understanding over the matter. Which was that if Layla doesn't show up in the next two days. Then they would leave without her. Jade tries to explain to them that two days maybe too late. That they all need to come to terms that Layla isn't coming back. That if they stay in this mansion any longer, they too will be missing along with Layla. Zorn try to calm Jade down & told her to be patient that Layla is going to show up? Jake agrees with Zorn & told everyone that this is nothing more than some practical nasty joke Layla is playing. Like she has done multiple times before? That if she doesn't show up in two days then they can alert the authorities. Which seem like a plan to everyone else. Except for Jade & Laura who thought otherwise. At that point, they decided to end the search & go back down to the dayroom. To see if they can catch anything unusual that happened last night on the surveillance camera. That may have to deal with the disappearance of Layla.

However, on the way down to the dayroom, Jill stops momentarily to look at a large painting on the wall. Which seem creepy of what she thinks of the picture in the painting. That seem so odd. Of what looks as if the eye in the painting is following her around. According to what she believes in her mind is happening. She then moves closer to the painting to get a better look. When from the corner of her eye she spotted a person dress in an all-black dress. Walking in one of the rooms down the hall from her. Jill in a loud tone of voice yell out the words "Hello"? As she thought that it was Layla playing her games again. Jill then begins talking as if the person in the black dress could hear her. While she heads for the room Layla went into? However, once Jill reaches the room she seem surprise that no one was there. That whoever it was had disappear from site. Which seems very strange of how someone can just vanish into thin air, without a trace? Which got Jill thinking about the story of the Carson's family. That maybe she seen the ghost of Ella Carson clear as day. Jill then begins to get scared as she started to back out of the room slowly. When suddenly, a hand grabs her shoulder! Jill at that point begun to scream as she jumps thinking the worse at that moment. Come to find out that it was Zorn making sure she was alright? As he told her not to stray away from the group. He then realizes that she seems all shaken up as if she had seen a ghost. As Jill explain to him that she had seen with her own eyes. The ghost of Ella Carson who came into this room. Who by the way vanish into thin air like it was nothing? Jill then told him that at first, she thought that it was Layla, but when she seen that the person had disappear. She knew right away who it was? Zorn told her that it is, okay? That she needs to rest for a bit.

CHAPTER 5

The Dead Zone

When the two of them arrive in the dayroom Jill told everyone what happened. That they need to leave this house immediately. Jade agrees with Jill & said that if they stay here any longer than they too will end up like Layla. Jason asks, Jill did she really see the ghost of Ella Carson walking around this place. Jill told him that she was pretty sure it was her prancing around in her black dress. Still in all, there were some who didn't believe that was the case. People like Jake, who insisted that it was Layla playing games with them. That she is taking this thing way too far. That she is not going to find it all that amusing when they leave her behind. He applied loudly enough so Layla can hear him, wherever she maybe? At that point, Jill became an emotional wreck. Since she wanted to leave. Christian & Lisa told Zorn that enough is enough. That something is not right with this place & that they need to leave, right now? Zorn on the other hand reminded everyone once again. That they are not leaving here without Layla. That they all need to stick with the plan & wait two days. That if she doesn't show up than, they were going to alert the authorities. Jason told Zorn to forget the plan that they are leaving now. Laura then grabs her keys to the car & told everyone who wants to go? To come along with her. That's when Jill, Jason, Christian, Lisa & Jade decided to leave without any explanation? Zorn on the other hand reminded them that they are under a contract. Which didn't matter to them as they slam the front door, as they walk out. However, once they reach the car it seems as if they ran into a little problem. As the car wouldn't start for some apparent reason. Which means that they are stuck here for the night without any other means of transportation. Besides the three other vans they came in that belongs to Zorn & his crew. Who decided to stay &

wait for Layla? Considering that now they don't have a choice but to wait those two days. Which upset Jill & Jade that they must stay here two more nights.

However, when they were on their way back to the mansion, they seen Zorn approaching them. To try & stop them from leaving. Knowing that he is responsible for them all & if anything should happen, he would be accountable for them. Which Zorn try to get the six of them to see that he is responsible for Layla. That if something did happen to her then the best thing for them to do is report it? That they need to be sure she is okay before they leave her behind. Which Jill & the others could understand coming from his standpoint? So, they all decided to go back into the mansion & stick it out for the remaining two days. When they got back inside of the mansion Laura told Zorn that her car wasn't working. He told her not to worry about it because he was going to look at it, first thing in the morning. However, later that night they all begin to experience some strange sounds coming from the mansion. The sounds of banging noises coming from all throughout the tower. Jake became frustrated & begin to yell out to Layla to stop playing games. That if she doesn't stop, he was going to come up there & make her. Elliot on the other hand seem calm & collected as if none of this bothers him in the lease. Which had Christian & Lisa thinking that he too feels as if this whole thing is a joke. Which didn't seem all that funny too them. The noise would soon come to an end, as everyone got ready for bed. Although, Jason, Christian & Lisa decided to stay in the same room with Jill. Considering that she would feel safe with her friends all together. The next morning, Christian woke up to seeing the witchcraft symbols made from twigs. Hanging on the walls that surrounded the room. Which wasn't there last night when they went to sleep. Christian then woke up the others to alert them about what is going on. Jill seems terrified about the whole setup as she & Lisa begin to get beside themselves. At that point, Jason begins to yell out for someone to come up to the room to see what is going on?

Zorn & the others heard their cries for help & came rushing up to the room. However, when Zorn & the others reach the room, they were stun about what they saw. As the camera men recorded each detail that goes on in this mansion. It seems as if no one could explain the phenomenal that has been taking place as of late. Except for Jade who instantly knew what the symbols meant? As she said time & time before that these symbols symbolize death. Which seem very odd to Jill & her friends as of what is happening at this point. With all the things they have gone through. Which seems as though something

19

seems off at this point. Almost as if Deja vu is starting to occur once again? As Jill couldn't get the thought out of her mind about that person using Eric Johnson's name to torment her. Almost as if someone in this group is trying to get inside of her head. As she had that feeling that someone from this group of people is connected to the email she received from this anonymous person. Claiming to be Eric's mentor who is seeking some sort of vengeance. According to what Jill believe is happening. Then suddenly? The word got around that Jake & Alex was missing in action. Which was another major problem. As there was no sign of Jake & Alex whereabouts in the mansion. Which started everyone to panic as of what is going on here? That there are two more people that is now missing. That there is no evidence on the surveillance camera that show anything out of the ordinary. That somehow, they manage to disappear without a trace. Which was the last straw for Jill & her friends as the writing was on the wall for them to leave. Elliot however, started laughing for no reason. Which had everyone wondering what in the world is so funny about this? Elliot then apologizes. And stated that something is in the air. As he walks out of the room. Which had them wondering what was that all about? Which led Seth Myers to argue the fact that since they have been here. All sorts of things have going wrong. That Todd Williams was telling the truth about this place. While they thought it was funny about what he was saying. That since they been here three of their friends have gone missing.

While experiencing some very unusual things like seeing ghosts & hearing noises throughout the mansion. Words alone doesn't describe how ironic things have gone. Since they step foot in this place. That one thing remains to be considered on what happened to their friends. Jill was convinced that it had something to do with the mansion. That what she saw wasn't her imagination. Being that this place is haunted with spirits hanging around. That something bad is bound to happened if they remain in this mansion. Which is something Jill & some of the others didn't want to stay around to find out. That now, is the time to leave while they still can before it is too late? Zorn had seen enough & elected to leave & come back with the police. Which seem like a waste of time considering of what good the police could do? Considering that they are not dealing with a homicide? They are dealing with ghost. Everyone at that point, seem clueless about what they should do? However, the first order of business is to get out of this place. Which should be their main concern as of now? The decision was then made that they would come back with the police. Since Zorn didn't want to leave behind any of his friends. However, before leaving Zorn told everyone that he needs to swing by the dayroom to inform Timothy about what is going on? However, once they got there, they found out that he too was missing. That there was no one around watching the surveillance videos. As things was now turning from bad to worse within the matter of minutes. Zorn at that point, begun to call out to Timothy to see if he was nearby, but all they heard was silence. However, just as they were about to leave the mansion. Zorn heard Timothy's voice on the walkie talkie. Which cause them to stop in disbelief that he was alive. Timothy had told them that he had wander off & slip into one of the secret compartments in the mansion.

That he is stuck there without any way out. Considering that he begs them to come & rescue him? Zorn told everyone to hold on that they need to find Timothy first, before leaving? Which bother some of them. Considering that no matter how hard they try, they just couldn't escape this place. That every time they try to leave, something always pulls them back in? Which created a serious problem for those who wanted to leave right than & there? As the decision had to be made on whether they would help look for Timothy or leave. In which, they decided to stick together for once? So that, no one else would turn up missing? Zorn told Timothy to try & pinpoint his location that they are on the way to get him. That he needs to tell them exactly which route he took so that they can find him. Timothy then begins to guide them to the center of the mansion. Where the building was off limits to the public. Which was block off by the police tape that stop them in their tracks. Which seem kind of weird at this point of how anyone could get by this. Without breaking the seal of the tape. Which had some of them second guessing this whole decision about entering? Considering that now they are entering a part of the mansion they have ever explore before? Where the murders supposedly have taken place years on in? It was at that point, where the connection got bad between Zorn & Timothy. As the walkie talkie had begun to static. Which put them in a tough position. Considering that they are now in deeply over their heads. As Jade begin to have a panic attack about being in a dark place. As she told everybody that this was a bad idea? About entering a place where they are not wanted? You couldn't imagine everyone's surprise when they enter a room. That was filled with all sorts of weird stuff & amongst that stuff was a rocking chair. That seems to be moving on its own without anyone in it? Which startled everyone as they try to rush out of the room. Without warning the door to the room slam shut, locking Alex inside.

CHAPTER 6

The Haunting Hour

It didn't matter how hard they try to pull the door open, it would not budge. As Alex begin to scream out in horror that the rocking chair had stop moving. He then begins to yell out the words "He is coming"! Panic begins to spread as desperation starts to set in? Words alone doesn't begin to describe the horror they must have felt. When they all heard the bloody screams of Alex being butcher by someone in the room. As the blood begin to come from underneath the door. As Jill & the others begin to panic when the other doors in the mansion begin to slam shut? Leaving them scrambling for a way out? That as they ran, the doors around them begin to shut close. Until they found themselves stuck in one of the mansion's suites. Jill & Jade became furious at Zorn & told him that this would happen? That now, they are trap here without any way out. However, it seem as if all is not lost, considering that they can still call the police. Which seems like a smart idea on Zorn's part. Which was the smartest thing he has thought of this far? However, it seems as though, their cellphones weren't getting through. That something was blocking the signal? Which was something they should have expected? Considering that the tower wasn't going to let them leave. Zorn then, told everyone not to panic because there is still a way out. If only they could locate one of the hidden passages in the room. That judging from the fact that they are in a suite. There is bound to be a hidden compartment some where's in the room. Elliot then suggested that everyone search the room for anything unusual. While searching the room Jason found an old picture of the Carson's family wearing their creepy costumes. In which, he shows the picture to Jill, Christian & Lisa? Jason would then ask" Zorn was this the family they were doing a documentary on? Zorn told them that they were indeed the family they were documenting. There was all sort of old stuff in the room that was all dusted up with lots of cobwebs hanging about.

Through their many years of experiencing horrific events, this is by far one of the worse encounter Jill & her friends experience. They then begin to hear footsteps coming down the hall. Headed toward the room they were in? Everyone at that point had begun to get scared. As something approach the door. What sounded like a couple of children messing around? As they all saw foot shadows running outside of the door. With the sounder of laugher from younglings running around. Which all turn serious when the children started to bam on the walls & doors. That scare the living daylights out of everyone. As they all begin to scatter to find a hiding place. Which scare the bejesus out of all of them, as Jill & Jade whimper for it to go away. Then suddenly, the noise stop? With the sounder of the children laugher retreating in the distance. Everyone at that point waited a few seconds before coming out from their hiding places. Everyone, except for Elliot & Seth who was no where's to be found in the room. Which was kind of strange in a way considering that they were just here a minute ago. That there is no way a person can just disappear into thin air like that? Without any explanation on where they went? Which was getting a little too weird for Jill & her friends. As the number keeps on decreasing on the people that they have left. Which was Zorn & Jade along with Jill, Jason, Lisa & Christian. At this point, Zorn had no idea what to do? As all the hope he had of getting out of the tower. Was now hopeless? That's when Jade turns all her frustration toward Zorn by letting him have it? Considering that this is all his fault if only he would have listened to her in the first place. At that point, Jill felt sorry for Zorn & told Jade to lighten up a bit. That they all are at fault. If only they would have listened to Mr. Todd Williams that had warn them about this place.

Which got Jason thinking that if he got out of this place alive than so can them. That there is a way they can get out of this place as well? Then suddenly, the door to the room crept open slowly. At first, they thought that it was trick that the door just suddenly open without warning. However, it was a way out which was all they could think about at that moment. Even though, they slowly made their way out of the room with caution. Knowing that anything can happened within the matter of second. Which can strike without warning? That all they need to do is stick together & not get separated from one another. Things at first, seem normal, but as they moved along. They started to experience some unholy things. Like sounds of doors being open & closed. As they move from one area to the next? Also, the sound of footsteps above them running around slamming doors. That stun each of them by reacting to the response by jumping at each thing that happens. However, nothing would prepare them for what would happen next? As Zorn started to pick up strange voices on his walkie talkie. As they heard all sorts of scary sounds on the walkie talkie. That just gave them the heebie jeebies? Then suddenly! They heard a loud thumping noise coming from behind them. That shook the entire room they were in. Which cause them all to run wildly through the mansion. As the noise was in pursue of them. It was at that moment? When Jade suddenly fell to the floor spraining her ankle. As the thumping headed toward her way. Which cause her to scream out in horror, as the noise approach her. Which cause Zorn to stop in his track to go back for Jade. Which was little too late for that? As Lisa & Christian try to convince him that it was too late to save her. While Jill & Jason kept on running. It seems as if Zorn had already made up his mind & decided to go back for Jade. Which gave Lisa & Christian no other choice, but to take off without him.

The two of them would soon catch up with Jill & Jason as they try to figure their way out of this nightmare. The four of them would soon run into a dead end. As they ran into a door that was barricaded & so was the windows. Which left them scrambling for a way out. As the thumping noise begin to get closer by the second. As the room begin to vibrate constantly as the sounds of terror approaches! Out of fear, the four of them begin desperately trying to pull off the wooden boards from the doors. Afraid of what they might see if they turn around to look at whatever it is approaching them. As desperation begun to kick in. As they started to panic uncontrollably, while not wanting to turn around to see what it is, that is after them? However, just as things was beginning to look grim for Jill & her friends. They suddenly, heard" Someone yell cut"? That's when everything stops including the noises? Only to turn around & find out that everyone was alive. As they seen the entire cast of the film applauding them for a job well done. It seems as if Jill & her friends couldn't find the words to describe how they feel at this present moment. As they were relief that it was all a joke, but still kind of stun? That once more they have been dupe by Zorn the Magnificent & his ability to create movie magic. By staging the whole thing to promote his new film project. A documentary about" The Five Senses of Fear"? The four of them were in disbelief as Jill still *couldn't bring herself to understand how did they do it? Zorn explain that this whole place is equip with the best equipment to stage a movie. That the tower itself is the movie set & that everyone was in on it? Except for the four of them. That there is a reason people refer to him as Zorn the Magnificent & they see why that is? Jason then asks, how in the world was they able to capture every moment on film? When his entire staff was always with him. Laura then applied" That they have a control room that does all of the editing? However, there was one thing Jill couldn't understand. Which was about the ghost of Ella Carson she seen.*

Zorn told her that it was Layla pretending to be Ella Carson walking into the room & than disappearing. Considering that the disappearance was the easy part. Being that the mansion was fill with all sorts of hidden passageways that was located throughout the mansion. Considering that the Carson's family was nothing more than an urban legend tale. That they made up too scare Jill & her friends. However, nothing would surprise them more than seeing who else was in on it? Like Todd Williams who was part of the documentary. By doing his part in trying to discourage them all from entering the Carson's tower. Jill & her friends seem amaze of how well they coordinated the whole act. Of not letting the four of them in on what they were doing? They even went as far as to throw in the mask of fear from the Face of Death masks. Which wasn't all that funny too the four of them. Which led to a misunderstanding on the subject? As Layla denied the fact that she had anything to do with that? In which, they all did? That had Jill, Jason & Christian thinking that someone was in on it, but was too ashamed to admit? Even though, they decided to look past the fact that the four of them was a pawn in Zorn's game. Which seem like no big deal to the four of them as it was just a form of entertainment? Zorn then turn his attention to the control room. As he wanted to introduce Jill & her friends to the rest of the crew. The control room however was in a secret room in the mansion. At the helm was Bobby Jackson, Will Fort & Jessie Lombardi. Who were the work horse of the film? Along with Timothy Jones who is also a member of the team. Who Jill & her friends already know? Being the editor of the film creates so much emphasis on what gets cut or add? That it was the job of the Four Horsemen to create magic. Which was the name given to them by Zorn. Bobby would then pull up the picture of the Carson's Family the same one Jason had showed Jill, Christian & Lisa?

CHAPTER 7

The Blackout

Which seem a bit up to date on the model in which the picture was taken. Then the one Jason found in the suite that look like it was taken in modern times. Bobby simply explains that he change the picture background to give it a more old time sinister look? That the people in the picture posing as the Carson's family. Was none other than Layla who played the mother, Jake who played the father & Jade, Alex, Seth & Laura who played as the children. After getting all the info they needed on the film. Jason, Christian, Jill & Lisa all headed back to the dayroom to discuss further matters about their contract. In the meanwhile, the cast & crew decided to throw a party to celebrate the film. They all had themselves a ball just living it up. However, just as things was getting exciting. A blackout occurred. Leaving everyone stranded in the dark which led Jade & Jake to reenact the beginning scene from the Twilight zone sitcom. Which annoyed everyone to the point where they all told the two of them to shut up? Which ended up with a howling that can from Alex. Who couldn't resist the temptation? As they started to pull out the flashlights to see what is going on. Seth told everyone that it must be the circuit breaker that could be the problem. So, Zorn got on the radio to ask it someone from the crew could go look? In which, they were already on the job as they speech? It seems as if some of the people in the dayroom wanted to explore the mansion in its entirety in the dark. Which seem like a bad idea to Jill & her friends considering that they may get lost. Zorn told them that everyone here knows the in's & out of this place. That they would be just fine? It seems like an eternity for them to get the lights back on. However, during that time it seem as if chaos ensued. As they heard all sorts of noises coming from throughout the mansion. Seems as though, it was no one other than the people who went exploring through the mansion.

Then just like that, the lights had cut back on. Without any hassle "whatsoever" from the engineer. Who went to see about the problem? It seems as if everything was back to normal. Until the engineer reported a dead body down in the cellar. That it was one of the crew members who is lying in a pool of blood with a knife stuck in his back. Which seem like some sort of prank being pulled? That everyone kind of look past considering that it was a joke that was being played on them. That judging from the engineer's voice, he seems sincere that this is serious. Not wanting to believe the hype Zorn & the others decided to go look for themselves. However, that feeling would soon change once they got down to the cellar. That they witness firsthand the murder of one of their colleagues. As reality begins to kick in that there is a murderer amongst them. Which seem so surreal to Jill, Jason, Christian & Lisa. Who begin to have that feeling once again? At that point, Zorn try reaching out to the control room to see what had happened, but there was no response? Which seem sort of weird considering that they weren't responding to his calls. So, they all decided to go up to the control room to see what is going on? To their surprise? They come to realize that Bobby & Jessie was dead. However, there was no sign of Will & Timothy no where's to be found. Which led them to a message that was left on the table. Underneath Bobby's hand? Which was written in Bobby's handwriting that said, "There's a Killer Amongst You"? Which instantly alerted Jill, Jason & Christian that this is no message. It was a sign that the killer left for the three of them to read. That whoever left this message was at the House of Horrors. Which got Jill thinking about the text message she receives from this anonymous person. Which left the message that said," This is where things get interesting"?

That judging from the e-mails she's been receiving from another anonymous person. Claiming to be Eric's mentor is probably the same person? Which got her thinking that things are now starting to get interesting. Considering that she must once again follow the signs? In hope, that it will lead to some answers on why this is happening? As Jill begin to explain to everyone that there must be another killer on the loose. Who knows about everything that has been taking place over the years? Which got the four of them thinking about the witness who Danny & Edgerrin James was referring too? Which didn't make no sense considering that this person had help them catch the two killers? And now, this person is trying to kill the four of them? Then suddenly, the thought had entered Jill's mind that someone here in the mansion lies the anonymous witness. That someone led them here under false pretense. Which turn their attention to Zorn who is the producer of this film project? He immediately denied any involvement in what's going on. Do to the fact that he was with them when the murder took place. Then suddenly, came busting through the door. Was Max Krueger the engineer who found the body. Making some strong assumptions about Layla who he spotted down in the cellar with blood all over her. Who he thinks killed one of the crew members? That the evidence should be on camera. Zorn then search the videos for anything concern the issue with Layla. However, a bit of a shocker grew on the face of Zorn. When there was evidence of proof that Layla was indeed down there fooling around with one of the crew members. That just before the lights went out, they all heard Layla say to the young man "Did he want to see something scary"? Then suddenly! the blackout occurs? That when Max turns the lights back on? He found the young man lying in a pool of blood with a knife stuck in his back. Which is proof that Layla is the one responsible for the murder?

Which is now all starting to come together, being that she was the one who left. The mask of fear behind so that Jill & her friends would get the message. That the four of them are still marked for death? However, what Max fail to mention was that when he spotted her in the cellar, she had on the Ella Carson costume. That she had a surprising look on her face as if she was stun by what she saw. Being that he caught her in the act? Deep down Jill, Jason, Christian & Lisa all felt as if something wasn't right the moment, they enter the mansion. That all they needed to do was to follow the signs. That it was almost too true that this whole thing was just a hoax. At that point, Lisa tries to get in touch with the police. However, her phone was block yet again from making any calls. Zorn would explain that the block calls was coming from a device. That they had setup to keep Lisa & Jill from making a false report. Considering that there was no real danger? That in order to make a call they must turn off the device. Zorn told Jill & her friends to come with him to search for the others to let know what is going on.? While Max go & turn off the device. So that, they can get the police down here. However, before going on their quest in search for the others cast & crew members. Zorn shut down the party that was going on in the dayroom. As he told the people that was there that there has been an emergency. That they all need to stay put until, he *gets back & to also. Remind the rest of the staff to stay put as well, when they return back from their site seeing. However, just as they were about to leave to search for the others. In came more terrible news as they heard a loud scream coming from some where's in the mansion.*

Which instantly got them thinking about the killer who may have struck again? Zorn then got on the radio to ask Max did he locate the device yet. In return, the response Zorn got. Wasn't from Max, it was from the killer who was on the two-way radio? Who suggested that they play a game called "Whodunit"? A game with many speculations on who is the killer? Which will raise the stakes on so many different levels of the game's truth concept? Which will intrigue the inquiring minds? Which was enough said for Jill as she nor her friends wanted no part of it? As they headed straight for the front door to leave. However, once they reach the gate to exit the premises. It seems as if someone lock them in. Which created a real problem? Since there was no other way out? Since the mansion was surrounded by a large wall. That seem impossible to get over, that had barbed wire on top of it. Which left them no other choice, but to face the music. That the killer made sure that they wouldn't leave. So, the plan now, is to find the device so that they can use the phone. However, once they reach the area where the device was? They found Max lying unconscious on the floor. Zorn try repeatedly to wake him up. It appears, he was, okay? However, when he awoken, he seems out of it? Claiming that someone place a piece of cloth over his nose filled with chloroform. That render him helpless. However, things would get even worse when there was no sign of the device. Which the killer may have in her possession. Seems as though, Layla is the one to blame. Speaking of which? Came the person of interest who right away pointed the finger toward Max Krueger. As Layla accuse him of murdering the young man she was with in the cellar. As he accuses her of doing the same thing. Which put them all at a crossroads about who is telling the truth?

CHAPTER 8

Terror in the Tower

However, it seems as if all eyes were on Layla as she tries to avoid being the center of attention. As Jill lay in on her about the faces of death mask. She had left for the four of them as a reminder. Yet alone, the stabbing of her co-worker to get her point across? Then by making a statement by creating a game called" Whodunit"? Which makes her a suspect in their eyes? However, it seems as if Layla had a few suspicions of her own, but first she would address Jill's questions? That for the second time she told them that she had no idea who place the mask of fear in the cellar to begin with. That just because she was in the cellar that night doesn't mean she was the one who done it? That they need to keep in mind that there were others who were down there as well. In which, she makes a strong point considering that it was a team effort? Layla also mentions that she had nothing to do with the young man being murder. That it is an issue they need to take up with Max Krueger. That all she knows was that one minute she was playing with him. When suddenly, the lights went out? Then the next? The lights had come back on with Max standing over the dead body. With her cover in his blood. And as far as the game goes? She doesn't have the slightest idea what they are talking about? Max, however, accuse her of knocking him out with chloroform. When he tries to retrieve the phone device. Layla replied" by telling him that there was no proof that his story was true. Considering that he maybe the killer who is trying to cover his own tracks. Which at that point, seems as if the door swung both ways? As they both made some valid points. That judging from Jill & her friends' perspective they both might be the killers? By trying to confuse them. By playing off each other in hope that their plan would work.

Zorn try to defuse the situation by asking Layla how in the world she knew they would be down here? Layla told him that she didn't know that they were down here. That she was coming for the phone device to call the police. Which got Lisa to notice something about Max? Which is how the killer knew he was trying to retrieve the phone device, in the first place? Which seem kind of strange of how it all went down? Almost as if the killer was just waiting on him to come into the room. So that, he or she could knock him out with chloroform. Which is a great point considering that there was no trace of evidence to show. Since he might have staged the whole thing. That for all she knows. He could have been the one on the other end of the walkie talkie who told them about the game. Which he denied doing? Of not having any involvement in none of what's been going on? That the killer is standing right in front of them. As he pointed in Layla direction? Which cause the two of them to bicker about who is the killer. Which got Jill thinking that this whole thing is stage. A front to lower their guard once again. That had the four of them wondering was this part of the film. That it was their job to create movie magic. While the four of them are subject to suffer the consequences of being humiliated. That the title of this film says it all? Which is the resulting name" The five senses of fear"? However, Layla & Max were certain that this was not part of the act? Jill & her friends knew that if this was part of the act. Then they weren't going to tell them anyway? Which really didn't matter to them anyway because Jason & Christian had about just enough of the suspense & wanted to leave. Which led Jason to grab & threaten Zorn that if he doesn't stop filming & let them leave. Then he was going to beat him into a bloody pulp?

Zorn told them that he doesn't know what is going on? That this is not part of the film. That there is a real killer on the loose. Jason wasn't sure whether he should believe him or not? So, he & the others decided to examine bobby & Jessie bodies to see if they are dead? However, once they got back to the control room, they found that the two dead bodies were missing. Which got Jill & her friends thinking that they are up to no good? Which turn their attention to the table where they found a script. A script that was identical to what was going on? Which infuriated Jason as he punches Zorn in the face for lying to them. About not being involve in another one of their schemes. That's when Max & Layla got involve & told Jason that it's not his fault. That someone decided to turn the film into a real-life scenario. As they both gave each other a look of disbelief? As they both started the blame game once again? Zorn told them

31

both to get a grip that there maybe someone else who is at fault. That there is someone playing off their emotions. By using the film as exploitation to get recognition. That if they just follow the script than it might led them to the killer. That judging from the script the next person to die. Was Todd Williams who was in on the act, but have no idea what is going on? As Zorn try to locate him on camera so that they can warn him that he is in danger? That by the time they located him it was too late. As they saw the costume of Tom Carson slowly creep up behind Todd Williams. Which was played by Alex Crawford who was underneath the costume. As they witness the ruthless stabbing of Todd Williams. Then suddenly the camera when off? They all then rush up to the room where Todd was killed? However, by the time they got up there it was too late. As they found him lying in a pool of blood. With a knife stuck in his back, the same as the young man. Only this time there was a note attach to the knife that said" Whodunit"?

At that point, they all seem confused on the matter considering that there was only one person who could have done this? That person being Alex Crawford? Who is using the alias name Tom Carson? It seems as if things are now starting to become serious? As now the attention was turn to Alex who committed a murder. They all then rush to find Alex before he can kill again. With a little bit of luck, they manage to find him tuck away in the corner of the room. Rocking back & forth facing in their direction. Holding a knife in one hand, while cradling an old teddy bear in the other. While humming the song Rock-a-bye Baby. Which creep out Jill & the rest of them as they begin to ease closer to him. At that point, Zorn in a hesitate voice begin to call out Alex name. To see if he was alright. Alex then stops rocking, once they got a few inches closer to him. Then suddenly! As Zorn lean in to ask Alex a question? He suddenly, jump up with the knife in his hand. While dropping the teddy bear on the floor. As he came at them in a violent manner swinging the bloody knife wildly? At that point, Jason went into survival mode. As he tries to wrestle away the knife from the deranged psychopath? It was a struggle indeed as the two fought over the knife. However, it was at that moment when Christian saw the opportunity to intervene. By socking Alex with a hard right to the back of the head. Which put an end to all the scuffling? Alex then took off the mask to see what the deal was with Christian hitting him on the back of the head. Then from out of no where's Zorn pull out a gun & told Alex to drop the knife. Which shock everyone that he even had a weapon on set. At that point,

Alex seems confused as he nervously asks his boss what is going on? That's when Layla asks him did, he killed Todd Williams. In which, he said" Yes"? As he told everyone that Todd is dead & that he killed him? They all were shocked by what they heard as he admits that he killed Todd Williams in cold blood. Which upset Zorn so much that he lost it? Not realizing what Alex just did.

Alex at that point, seem as if he didn't care what was said about him? As he tries to understand what the big deal was. That's when Jason grabs him by the back of the neck & shoved him into the room where Todd dead body was? Which was a shock to even Alex? As he tries to explain to them that it wasn't him that did this? As Zorn told him not to deny the fact that it was him who did this? That they all heard him confess to the murder, which came from his own mouth. Alex admitted that the killing was all stage that there was no way he could kill someone for real. Especially, with a fake knife he had use to up the antics to make it seem more real. Jason grab the bloody knife from Alex hands to examine it? As it turns out that he was telling the truth about the knife? However, it still wasn't enough to get him off the hook. Since he could of switch the two knives. To make it seem like he was innocent. However, he was still held accountable for the costume. Which was a dead giveaway? That he was the only one wearing that costume at the time. Alex swore it wasn't him, as he told them that it could have been someone else wearing the costume. To make it seem like it was him? In which, he makes a great point considering the letter that was place on Todd body that says" Whodunit"? That they must consider everyone as a suspect at this point. Which didn't look good for Jill & her friends. As they didn't know who to trust? Which could be the case in Layla situation with the young man who was killed, while in her presence? Which so happens when the light's shut off. Leaving two possibilities that either of them could be the killer. Along with someone else who maybe involve? Which is the question as of now? Which didn't set well with Jill & her friends. That now, there is a psychopath some where's pretending to be someone they are not? Which plays in the hands of the killer. Who is using the game" Whodunit" to express the true nature of psychology? That the four of them must always keep their guard up. Words alone doesn't even begin to describe the mind games that the four of them had to endure. That trying to figure out who the killer is? Is sort of like trying to find a needle in a haystack? Which was one way to put it? That now, there will be some trust issues along the way, as they move forward.

CHAPTER 9

The List

That one thing they must keep in mind, is that someone in this mansion is the killer? Considering all the speculation that has been going around about who is the perpetrator that makes it even harder to consider? Just who is the one responsible for this mix up? That the list is growing substantially large in the death toll. Which is a reminder to Jill & her friends. That they need to do something to get control of the situation before it gets out of hand. However, things were really starting to get out of hand. As one of the crew members came running up to them screaming hysterically. That someone from the crew has been killed? At that point, Zorn didn't know whether he was acting or telling the truth. That judging from the way he was acting. It was sort of difficult to tell whether he was in character? Of trying to sell the idea that it was all a front to lure them in. By making them believe that someone has been murder. As he explains to them that he witnesses first-hand the brutal murder of one of the co-workers. Who was stab to death by two individuals wearing some awfully creepy costumes? In which, they turn their attention toward him, soon afterwards? As they started to chase him down, but lucky for him, he got away? Which sound like a sincere story to Jill & the others. As they demanded to know the whereabouts to where this occurs. So, they can determine for themselves whether this was a false alarm or not? However, just as they were headed toward the place where the dead body was? In came a surprise, that caught them all off guard. That as the young man went to open the door to one of the rooms. The killer appears wearing Ben Carson costume who without warning went to stabbing the young man. Several times in the stomach who fell onto

Zorn pinning him to the floor. Jill & Lisa try to help Zorn by trying to pull off the young man's body, but their attempt to rescue him fail.

As the killer came in for the kill, in which Jason pull the two of them back just in the nick of time. However, another killer appears behind them. Who grab a hold to Layla & pull her into one of the rooms? The doors around them then started to slam shut. As they all begin to run wildly through the mansion. Leaving behind Layla & Zorn who probably was killed by the two killers. Although, they thought to themselves that it was probably all stage to begin with? Even though, they weren't going back to find out. Which created a real problem for Jill, Jason, Christian, Lisa & Max who didn't know what is real & what is not? Almost as if they were wedge between a double-edged sword? Which can affect the outcome to the game? As of who is doing what, & who all is involve in the scandal? Max had just about enough of the nonsense & elected to go back for Layla & Zorn. Christian thought that it was a bad idea for him to go back. Not knowing the circumstances he's putting himself in. Which really didn't matter to Max who just couldn't stand around doing nothing? While his friends are probably in need of some help? Which seem like the right thing to do? Considering that things may not be, what they seem to be? However, just as Christian & the others was getting ready to follow Max into the other room. The door that separates the two room's slam shut. Leaving Max to defend for himself. That just before the door slam shut. Christian tries to warn him that the killer was headed his way. At that point, Max begins to yell for them to open the door. In which, they couldn't as the door seem stuck. However, it seems as if Max wouldn't go down without a fight. As he told the killer to bring it on? While Christian & the others try desperately to get the door to open. Before it was too late? In the meanwhile, Jill looks through the keyhole on the door the see what was going on, between the killer & Max. As the two struggles over dominance to see who would come out on top? Which turn disastrous when another killer in a costume appear that went for the kill? By killing Max in the process, while he was engaging in a fight with the other killer. In which they gang up on him? However, nothing would prepare Jill for what would happen next?

That what seem like a friendship between the two killers would suddenly turn disastrous! When one of the killer's decided to kill the other by stabbing whoever it was underneath the costume too death? Which had Jill holding her head about what just happened? As Jason, Christian & Lisa wanted to know what happened? Jill then started to explain what had occur while they were trying to open the door. Which didn't make no sense whatsoever of why one killer would kill the other killer? When both killers killed Max Krueger? It would seem as if something fishy is going on around here. That something doesn't quite add up here according to Lisa's theory? Then suddenly, the door opens with little speculation that it is Will Fort & Timothy Williams who is doing this. Considering that they have control over the equipment. Which makes them a liable source considering their hand in all of this? That they were in the control room when Bobby & Jessie was killed? However, they can't rely on that fact either. Considering that they too disappear into thin air. Which didn't make no sense to them as of why this is happening. Considering that there are so many different leads on this case. As of who could be the killer. Which makes things difficult for Lisa, Jill, Christian & Jason? As they try to make somewhat of an understanding about what is going on. As Jill reminded them all that they must "follow the signs" to get a better understanding about what is going on here? In the meanwhile, Jill found herself completely disturb. When they enter the room next to them & saw that there was no sign of Max nor the person in the costume that was killed. To be found no where's in site? That their dead bodies had also disappear into thin air? That the only evidence that was left was the blood on the floor. Which states the obvious that there is something wrong here? Considering that dead bodies just doesn't up & disappear like that? Without some sort of explanation that would clarify some facts on the matter.

However, there lies a trace of evidence as they saw a blood trail leading to the hallway. Almost as if someone had been dragging a dead body. Which instantly got them thinking about Max & the person in the Carson costume. They follow the trail all the way to the end of the hallway. Where they spotted the legs of Max being pulled into a room by someone. Jason & the others rush to see who it was pulling Max into the room? Come to find out that it was Elliot Smith? Who seem surprised to see the four of them? As he tries to explain to them that things are not what they seem? That he found Max's body lying in the middle of the floor. In which, he trips over trying to get away from the killer. Jill asks him, what happened to the other body that was down there with Max. Elliot told her that there was no other body? Which sort of makes her feel suspicious that he is hiding something. That she knows good & well that there was another body along with Max. That was wearing the costume of Diane Carson who was killed along with Max. By a person wearing a Rachel

Carson costume who killed them both. Elliot then recalled that it was indeed a person wearing the costume of Rachel Carson who was chasing him. That person being Laura who was wearing the costume of Rachel Carson. Which all sounds like a bunch of nonsense to Jill & her friends. Considering that his story seems a bit off, being that he was trying to throw them off? Since he was caught red handed. Who try to cover his tracks by lying to them about what happened? Which all seems too weird of how Max body was found & not the killer wearing the costume. That he is the only person that suddenly appear out of no where's. When the only killer in the area appears to be him. That there is no one else around he can blame for the two murders. Elliot tries to convince the four of them that he is being setup by someone, in particular. Which created more stress on Jill & the others as they try to figure this thing out? Considering that they didn't know whether Elliot was telling the truth or lying to them.

Which turn their world upside down as they try to make sense about what is going on? Words alone doesn't begin to describe the agony the four of them had to endure. On trying to solve this mystery. However, things would get even interesting when Christian spotted a message that was written on the wall in the room. Which was written in cold blood that say's "Who's Next"? Which was an indicator that they must figure out who's next on the list to die? That judging from the blood on Elliot's hands tells the story. Which was a dead giveaway that it must have been him who wrote it? Which had the four of them thinking that it was getting so that they couldn't trust anyone, at this point? As they all turn to run away from this guy. As Elliot try to go after them by telling them that "he could explain"? Which didn't set well with Jill & her friends. As they got as far away from him as they could. Christian then suggested that they get the hell out of this mansion. Before they all end up dead? As Jason told Christian how can they leave when there is no way out of this place? Which brings up a good question considering that this was all a setup to lure them here. That judging from everything that has happened. It would seem to them as if this whole thing has been stage. That someone had plan this whole thing? They just didn't know who it was? Tension had begun to build as they scramble to look for another way out. Hoping that they find a secret passage that would lead to the outside. As it turns out that finding a secret compartment wasn't that hard to find. Considering that all they needed to do was to know where to look? However, they knew that entering through the hidden compartment would be highly risky. Considering that there could be danger up ahead. That there's a good chance they may run into the killer. Who loves entering through the hidden compartments to get around easier? It seems as if the secret passages lead them to a place where they didn't want to be? Which was down in the dark cellar where it all begun?

CHAPTER 10

The Beginning of the End

Which is where everything begun, starting with the faces of death mask. Which so happens to be the mask of fear which has to deal with the title of this film. Which is" The five sense of fear"? That if Jill is correct than they basic the film around Danny Burton & Edgerrin James philosophy about fear. Which means that someone must have known about the two killers. Which got them thinking about the witness who is anonymous? Which could be the one using Eric's name as a decoy to finish what Danny & the Sandman started? However, the thought that cross their minds was the fact that this person was the one who got them killed. Which didn't make no sense as of why this person would continue with the murders? Which was one thing they couldn't bring themselves to understand? However, there was a good chance that someone in the mansion is the anonymous person they have been searching for. Who may have some answers for them about why this is happening? That judging from the list of people that are enlisted in this film project. That anyone of them could be the mystery killer or killers? Which got Jill thinking of another scenario that may have some value in the case. Which got her thinking about the e-mail she receives from this anonymous person. That said," Beware the bucket list, in result to the fear of death"? Which got her thinking about the people that are on the killer's list? That there is some sort of bucket list that she needs to beware of? In result, she would face the fear of death. Which is where the mask of fear comes in? Knowing that the fear of death is consider as the foundation for the faces of death masks. That the e-mail was some sort of warning to her that there is trouble in her future. That all she needed to do was to follow the signs that was given to her. That states the obvious that there is trouble brewing in the midst, which she fails to pick up on? That now, they are left with no idea what to do? That the object of the game is to keep looking for clues that will lead them to the killer? Sort of like they are being tested in a way. To bring some sort of knowledge about the reality of having to rely on instinct alone. If they want to solve this puzzle? That they would have to do so, without get killed in the process. That the curse remains in effect to all that is present. As Jill wonder does this still have something to do with Jason?

No matter what, they will have to get to the bottom of this mystery? As they made their way through the cellar & up the stairs to the dayroom. Where they found Layla alive along with Seth Myers. Who they thought was dead when the killer grabs a hold to her? As it turns out that the killer was none other than Seth Myers who was in character at the time. Which was a lucky break for Layla? However, the same couldn't be said about Zorn who they believe is dead. Which brought up the subject about Max? As Layla wanted to know what happened to him. Jill told her that he was killed by Elliot who is the killer. Which to Layla seem a bit surprising to know that Elliot is the killer. As she probably figures that maybe he was setup. By the same person who try to frame her. Which seem likely considering that there were two killers at first. Until one of the killers gets killed by the other. In which, it seems that way to Jill? That for all she knows that part could of be stage. As Lisa told Jill that she needs to be sure that happened? Because things may not be what they seem? After all, the name of the game is" Whodunit" which means that they would have to follow the signs to figure out who the killers are? That there is variety of people that they must choose from? Which didn't take long to sort out, as the cast of the film begin to meet up in the dayroom. That being Laura, Jade, Alex, Jake & Elliot? Who wanted to know what is going on with the film. Being that someone is taking their job way too seriously? That they need to address the elephant in the room that being that there is a killer amongst them. Who is wearing the costumes of the Carson's Family? To murder the crew of the film by making it look like it's one of them. Which is where the problem comes in? As the seven of them started the blame game by accusing one another about who is the one that is doing all the killing. Which confuse Jill & her friends about who is to blame considering that they all made some valid points about one another? That there is a good chance that one of them are putting up a front to throw them off? By using the cast as a liability to create havoc. By using each one of the Carson's family costumes that is worn by the cast to shake things up a bit. On the fact that one of them is the real killer.

Which is where all the confusion comes in, being that they couldn't tell which of them are lying? That's when Jason came up with a solution that would resolve this whole issue? Which is that they stick together & not get separated from one another. Which shouldn't be a problem considering that none of them admits to being the killer? That if they work together as a team than they can catch the killer together. Which seem like a splendid idea to Lisa as she agrees with Jason. However, there still were some speculations on the matter. Considering that there are some trust issues that needed to be attended too? That there was no way some of them was going to walk around with the killer in their midst? That the killer may not be one of them according to Christian. Who had other suggestion on who it maybe? That there was still the possibility that Timothy & Will Fort maybe the one's responsible? That the two of them could be the one's running the show. That after all, there are the ones who engineer this place. Which bring up a good point considering that the two of them are no where's to be found? That the attention suddenly turns towards Timothy Jones & Will Fort as the two prime suspects? As the search was on to find the two of them. They search high & low for Will & Timothy but had no luck with finding them. Which seem almost impossible that the two of them were able to disappear without a trace. However, they did manage to come across Zorn's gun that was lying on the floor. Where he was last seen before the killer got a hold to him. As they started to back track their steps to see if they could come across something important, like a sign from the killer? It was then, when Jade came across some headshots of them. Lying on a nightstand in a folder that had each person's photograph from the cast to the crew in it? Considering that it was a step in the right direction. As the note in front of the folder read" Whodunit"? Which was indeed a sign from the killer? Who recommended that they take a closer look at the people in this line up?

That judging from the marker that was sitting long side the folder it seems as if the killer. Wanted Jill & her friends to X-out the dead suspects from the potential ones. That as the numbers of the decease decline the more of their chances go's up on finding the actual killer or killers? That from everyone's standpoint on who is alive & who is not? Played a significant role in the games true concept. On whom potentially could be the killer in their midst? That time is growing closer to their death as of which person is the killer? Just as they

41

thought that everything was okay to go on. They suddenly found themselves stranded in the dark. As all the lights in the mansion went out. Which proves to be crucial as they scramble out of desperation to find each other. They would then hear Laura scream in horror as if something was happening? As they had a hard time locating her in the dark. Yet alone one another for that matter? As they didn't know who was who scrambling around in the room. Everyone then started to panic as they had no idea what is going on? Then the lights suddenly, came back on? However, while looking around to see if everyone was, okay? They discover that Laura had been murder. Which raise a few eyebrows on the subject? That whoever murder Laura is still in the room with them. That the killer waited until the perfect moment to strike? That the timing of it all was just too precise to stage something of this magnitude. Considering that this was the killer's plan from the start. Considering that there is a strong possibility that someone in this group is working with Will & Timothy. Which arouse everyone suspicion that there is a killer hiding amongst them. That started some finger pointing between the cast on who is the killer? That ended up with them splitting up from the group. As tension begin to grow within the group. However, Jill, Jason, Christian & Lisa elected to stay together. As the four of them was skeptical about which of the cast is the killer?

Jade & Elliot wanted to tag along with Jill & her friends, but Jill felt that it wasn't a good idea. Considering that they didn't know who to trust at this point? Lisa then took the folder with the pictures in it. To figure out which one of them is doing what? That judging from the conversation she had with each of them early on. Explains a lot considering where each of them stands? That the argument can be made that each of them could fit the description of the killer? That their personality says it all about each one of them. That neither of them couldn't be trusted. The discussion was then made that they should take a stroll down to the control room to see if Will & Timothy are down there? However, on their way down to the control room. The lights begun to flicker off & on making it difficult for Jill & her friends to make their way through the mansion. They then begin to hear footsteps tagging along behind them. However, when they look back to see who it was? It was very dark as they barely could see who it is, creeping around them. Immediately, the thought had entered their mind that it was the killer. Who was getting ready to pick one of them off? It was sort of like a game that when they stop moving. The footsteps would stop moving as well & when they started to walk again? The footsteps would move along with them. As it was just a repeatedly cycle of following in Jill & her friends' footsteps. Until Jason got fed up with this ordeal & decided to do something about it? Keep in mind that the lights still have an influence them. Which has disabled their senses to see what is going on? Which is one of the many tricks Will & Timothy has up their sleeves. With everything that has gone on. It seems as if the cameras were still rolling. That the film is still a go ahead to capture movie magic, in a different light? Starring the killer who is using the documentary as a platform to create awareness to Eric Johnson's situation. According to Jill's theory about the motive behind the killer's actions? That judging from the scenery something was about to happened. As the four of them begin to brace themselves for what's is about to take place?

CHAPTER 11

The Hunt

Words doesn't even describe how afraid the four of them must have felt? When a shadow appears in the distance that was approaching them. As the footsteps slowly crept toward them in a very heart pounding moment. That just as the moment of truth was about to occur. From out of no where's! Came running toward Jill & Lisa was the killer dress in Sam Carson's costume. With a hook in his hand that was headed straight in Jill & Lisa's direction. However, in the nick of time came some shots from a gun. That killed the person dress as the killer. As it turns out that the shots came from Elliot who saved the two of them from being killed by the killer? Along with him was Jade who was the one's that follow Jill & her friends. That they were the ones who was following them all along. Who had to intervene by saving Jill's life? At that point, Jill seems grateful that they were there? Considering what may have transpired if they didn't follow them. Which was a good question as Jason wanted to know why they was following them in the first place. Jade told them that they wanted to help them by finding out who the killer is? That after all? They too are being hunted by this person who is looking to kill the two of them. That by the grace of God they finally got him or her? Christian went over to the dead body to uncover who it is, behind the mask? To their surprise it was none other than Timothy Jones who was gasping for air. Who seem a bit shock about what happened to him & scared at the same time? It seems as if he was trying to mumble a few words. As pointed his finger in Elliot's direction. Eventually, in the end, he would succumb to his injuries, as he took his final breath. At that point, the lights had stop flickering. As the question now, that was on everyone's mind is why was Timothy pointing at Elliot? Almost as if he was trying to say something to him. Which really didn't matter do to the fact that they have killed one of the killers. Now all is left, is Will Fort who is teaming with one of the casts? Which got Jill & her friends thinking about Elliot who Timothy pointed out. Before he died who was killed by Elliot in cold blood. Which didn't feel right to the four of them that something feels a bit off? That just by looking at him makes a statement. As they all saw a look of satisfaction on Elliot's face. Almost as if he was relieved that he killed Timothy? That judging from his body language he shown no remorse whatsoever, for Timothy in the least.

As Lisa took Elliot to be a stone-cold killer considering that it was foolish of him to killed Timothy. When he could have injured him enough to where he could talk to them. Considering that there was something he wanted to say. Which was something containing to Elliot? Which could have been something important that may have been something useful. Jade told Lisa that Will may have some information about what is going on? That after all, Will & Timothy was working together as a team anyhow? Which led them to go down to the control room to find Will Fort. However, once they got down to the control room. They found no sign of Will no where's to be found as they look to the cameras. To see if they could spot the killer lurking around the mansion. Instead, they found Will Fort on camera walking around one of the rooms. They saw that he had a walkie talkie in his hand. So, they decided to get in touch with him through the radio. As they found a walkie talkie sitting on the charger. They have got in touch with Will as he was in search for Timothy. Which he mentions? Jade told him that Timothy was dead. That Elliot killed him in self-defense. That he was trying to kill Jill & Lisa being that he was the killer. That they know just as well what the two of them been up too? Will told them all that he was no killer & so wasn't Timothy. That the two of them was under the impression that some of the cast members was the killer. That the reason Timothy had on the costume was to investigate the cast members by disguising himself as the killer to get to the bottom of this nightmare. As he had a few leads on who the killer maybe? Which was the break everyone was waiting for. However, Will told them to stay put that he was on his way down to the control room. That he didn't want to broadcast the name over the air. No telling who maybe listening. Will then warn them that there may be a killer in the area, but before he could say anything else. The radio went out. Then suddenly, the lights became a factor once again. As the lights begun to flicker at a rapid pace leaving the six of them at a disadvantage. As all the cameras in the control room went blank. Elliot then prepares himself with Zorn's gun as they all approach the door to the room.

However, before Elliot could open the door, in comes walking in was Alex Crawford. With a bizarre look on his face, as Jade asks him what was wrong. It seems as if something was troubling him as he took a few steps forward only to collapse into Jason's arms. Who was standing right next to Elliot? As it turns out that Alex had been stab multiple times in the back. As Jason gently laid him on the floor, while telling him that it's going to be okay. At that point, everyone seems so busy attending to Alex. That they had forgot all about the killer who was standing in the doorway wearing the Ben Carson costume. That caught the eye of Jill as she begins to scream. Which got everyone's attention, as they begin to turn around to see what is going on? The killer then launches at Elliot & Jason went the room went completely dark. Almost as if the killer time it perfectly. Which caught the two of them off guard that ended up in disaster. As there were shots fired in the room from Zorn's gun. As there was some confusion on what is going on? Somehow, Lisa manages to get a hold to a flashlight. Which help a lot on seeing what is going on around them. As it turns out that the killer was no where's to be found. Although, it was hard to tell whether Elliot shot the suspect or not? Do to the fact that the killer manages to escape into the darkness. At that point Jade told Elliot to shut & lock the door. So that the killer doesn't catch them off guard again? Elliot on the other hand wanted to go after the killer to see if he shot suspect & to see who is behind the Ben Carson mask. Then it occurs to them all, that the killer is none other than Will Fort. Who had told them that he was on the way to the control room? Which made Elliot eager to go after him even more. Lisa told Elliot don't be foolish, that all he is going to do is fall right into the killer's gameplan. By getting himself killed in the process. At that point, Jade & Elliot wanted to know what was Lisa & her three comrades gameplan.

Since the four of them are the experts in this sort of situation. Jason had then suggested that they all stay put, for the time being. Until they can come up with a solution that would help them in the long run. While standing around waiting to come up with some sort of concept that would help them? Jill & the other notices a funny smell coming from the air vent. Come to find out that it was some sort of sleeping gas that knock them all out one by one. As they all scramble toward the door to escape the gas. However, it seems as if someone *jammed the door from the outside. Leaving them all to collapse in the room. However, when Jill, Jason, Christian & Lisa awoke from their slumber? They found out that Elliot & Jade was missing & that the door to the room was open. Which seem very odd to the four of them as they could have sworn that the two of them had been knock out from the gas also? Which brings them to the question that something doesn't add up about their disappearance. As they try to make sense about what is going on. As of why the four of them are still alive. If somehow the killer manages to get into the room they was in? Which had the four of them questioning themselves about what all went on? While they were asleep? Which brought their attention to the table where they found a handwritten letter from the killer. Explaining that things aren't what they seem? That the four of them must figure out whodunit? Considering that the people they think are dead are not & that there's a good chance one or a few of them are playing possum. That they must keep in mind that someone from the cast & crew of this film lies the killer or killers? That it is up to the four of them to figure out who amongst the bunch is the perpetrator?*

That just because a person appears to have been stabbed or shot doesn't mean it couldn't of been staged? That after all, it is a movie? Which means there are all sorts of deception being played right before their very eyes. Which got them thinking about Alex Crawford who body was also missing? That there's that chance he could be the one faking his death? Which could also be said about Zorn & the rest of the cast & crew who maybe the one's behind this madness. That based on the clues giving by the killer. One or a couple of them are behind the masks of the Carson Family getup? Which led the four of them to the three Faces of Death masks that was lying side by side from one another on the end of the table. Which is a dead giveaway that someone knew about their experience that have to deal with the Faces of Death murders? That they are willing to bet that the killer is none other than this anonymous person. Who left Jill those nasty comments on social media? Who is using Eric Johnson's name as a cover up? Who also left the message that" This is where things get interesting"? Which was the message they have gotten before at the House of Horrors? Which was the thing that they couldn't bring themselves to understand? Of how it all relates to the story? Something that they should have expected knowing that there is always that possibility that one or two killers remains anonymous. Who are looking to seek vengeance against those who are wrong? Which is where the Faces of Death masks come in? Which got the four of them strongly considering that someone from the crew is putting up a performance. Who wants to get their point across by getting them to follow the signs? Which could be good or bad for them. Which would make an amazing story for their book. To finally put the missing pieces together to the jigsaw puzzle.

CHAPTER 12

Staging the Plans

It appears the four of them got the memo about what's going on with how things present itself. Of what they can expect from then on end about who can they trust. That they must come to terms that everyone is a suspect. Until they can prove otherwise that says differently. However, while in the control room waiting to see what happens next. It seems as if someone was trying to get in touch with Jill & the others on the walkie talkie. As it turns out that the person trying to get in touch with them was none other than Elliot. Who disappear from site when they regain consciousness from being knocked out by some sort of gas? Who sounded as if he was in a panic about something? Almost as if he was being chase by someone who he thinks is the killer. As it turns out that it was just a false alarm considering that it was just the sound effects. That seem all too real as Jill & the others knew that feeling all too well. Considering that they when through it earlier. However, it seems as though Elliot has gotten a hold of the device that can turn the signal back on. So, that they could get a hold to the police. The plan now was to meet him in the basement so that they all could be there together. When they make the call to the police. In which case sounds like a plan to Jill, Jason, Christian & Lisa. Who by the way wanted to know if Jade was with him? Elliot responds by telling them to beware that there's a killer on the loose. That anyone could be the killer in disguise as the potential suspect in order to conceal one's identity. Which gave Lisa the impression that Elliot was the one who may have written the note to them that all is not what it seems to be. Instead of the killer whom they assume wanted them to follow the signs as usual. As they made their way down to the basement to meet up with Elliot who has the device to clear the signal so that they could call for help? It seems as if the flashlights seem useful in finding their way through the dark tower in order to get to their destination. However, while trying to find their way through the dark tower. The four of them begin to experience some very unusual things. Like how they would hear footsteps tagging along behind them in the dark. However, when they shine the flashlight in the area where they would hear the footsteps. It seems as if nothing was there. However, what made it even scarier was the slamming of the doors. Follow by the laugher of what sounded like children playing all around them in the dark. Which has the four of them spook out of their minds. Figuring that the killer maybe nearby stalking their every move. By using the special & sound effects in the background to intensify the scene even more. However, nothing would prepare them for what would happen next. As they heard a voice on the walkie talkie saying to them to beware the bucket list for it will result in death for one of them. Which alerted them all to be aware of their surroundings. Not knowing what to expect to happen. Which seems to be the case as of now with all the stuff that is going on. That it is hard for them to predict when & where the killer may strike. Considering that they must be very careful not to play into the killer's hand. However, once they reach the door that led to the basement. It seems as if everything stops around them including the footsteps. However, once they made their way down in the basement. They found a body lying on the basement floor face down with a Tom Carson costume on. Which seems suspicious to Jill & the others of what to make of it. Whether it's part of a prank or that someone is seriously in trouble. Without thinking twice about it, Christian went over to check on the person to see if whoever it is, are okay. Figuring that whoever it maybe could have been in the same predicament they were in with the gas. Lisa then told Christian to be careful considering that they don't know the circumstance this person maybe in. Christian then bent down to see who this person was underneath the mask. However, when he turns around the body to see who it was. They heard the basement door slam shut which scare the living daylights out of them. As Jason took it to be Elliot coming to meet them, as he went up to meet him. However, when Lisa turns her focus toward the body. She seen that whoever it was dress in the Tom Carson costume has risen with a knife. To claim the next victim which was Christian who was unaware at the time. Who was looking to see if it was indeed Elliot who Jason was going to meet? However, nothing would prepare him for what would happen next? As Lisa shouted out in horror for Christian to turn around? Only to see the killer going straight toward his torso with the knife. In which the killer pulls him straight toward the sharp object. Stabbing him multiple times in a violent rage before shoving him aside like a piece of carcass. In which the killer arises from the floor to claim another victim. Which seems to be Jill as Lisa tries to intervene by protecting Jill from the killer. However, the killer would push Lisa aside like some rag doll since the killer has Jill in his or her site. The killer was moments away from claiming its next victim. That is until Jason came along & pull her away in the nick of time before the killer could get to her. However, when Jason when to protect Jill from the killer. It seems as if the killer had disappeared into the dark basement when Jason tries to find whoever it maybe with the flashlight. Jill & Jason then went over to check on Lisa who seems to be heartbroken over Christian's death. As Jason told Jill & Lisa that they have to go, before the killer returns. Which seems very hard to do when someone they love is some where's lying in the basement dying. In which case there was nothing more they could do for him. As Jill & Jason had to almost drag Lisa from the basement. Words doesn't even begin to describe how they all must feel at this point. To lose someone who has been through this many times before without so much as a scratch. As Jason made it his priority to see that this person pays for what he or she done to Christian. Which was Jill & Lisa's main priority as well to see to it that this person pays for his or her crimes. That they are no longer going to be a victim in the killer's eyes. That for once they are going to stay & see this thing through even if it kills them. That for once they are tired of running considering that it all ends here. As Jason got on the walkie talkie to deliver the message to whoever is listening on the other end. Which brought his attention to Elliot who was a no show when it came time for him to meet them in the basement like they plan. As Jill told Jason that he must consider the fact that he too may have been a victim of circumstances. Since Jason was unable to get in touch with him on the walkie talkie. However, Jason would get a respond back on the walkie talkie. Although, it wasn't the responds they were looking for. As they heard the killer's voice on the other end saying to them that there's a killer amongst them. Who must beware the bucket list, in result to the fear of death? As the killer add that if they want to know who kill their friend than they must find out Whodunnit? That they should be a little more aware about who they surrounded themselves with? That there's a good chance that the killer maybe someone from their past. Which put things in prospective as of who they must consider as a potential suspect. *That they were going to find the one's responsible even if it means researching everyone's background that have deal with this project. As Lisa related a final message to the killer to prepare themselves for what is coming. Now that they know where they stand as far knowing that it is someone from their past. Who is the killer only this time they haven't got a clue about what the motive maybe this time around? As they try to figure out who wants them dead. That for all they know it could be a copycat killer who is seeking attention by recreating what Danny & Edgerrin James establish. By finishing what the two of them started by doing a film about the resurrection of the Faces of Death controversy starring the four of them. Considering that someone decided to turn a fictional story into a real-life event. By turning the film into a Whodunnit sort of scenario where the plot of the story is to draw some attention by making headlines. On the mystery containing to how this film resonates with how it links back to Danny & Edgerrin James persona. Only this time around the patterning would change in how the killer would adapt to his or her surroundings. By using the Carson's family costume use by the six actors. As a decoy to make it seem as if one of them is doing the killing which could be the case. However, there still a chance that the killer maybe one of the crew members or even Zorn himself aka Zack Crenshaw. That one of them is the killer in disguise. That it is only a matter of time before Jill, Jason & Lisa discovers who they are? That they are determined to find the person responsible for Christian's death. That they owe it to him to seek justice in his name. As it turns out that they didn't have to wait that long to start their investigation. As they gotten a call from Will Fort on the walkie talkie. Claiming that he needs to speak with them concerning the issue with Timothy. As Will could have sworn that Timothy was dead according to them. Which didn't make no sense as he told them that he just spoken with Timothy on the walkie talkie a few minutes ago. Who suggested that he meet him in the basement to turn on the emergency lights? So, that he can look at the cameras to see if he can find them. So, that they could go over the plans for the next scene.*

CHAPTER 13

The Guilty Party

Which seems like a red flag to Jill, Jason & Lisa who told Will Fort that they don't know who told him that, but Timothy is dead for sure. However, Will insisted that it was Timothy's voice he heard on the walkie talkie. As Will told them that the whole thing was stage that Elliot didn't really shoot him. That according to Timothy the bullets were blanks. That at the time he was wearing a blood vest to make it seem real. Which would explain why Elliot didn't seem all that concern about Timothy wellbeing. However, they still were in a conflict about what they read on the letter concerning that things are not what they seem. That they need to be aware that there is an actual killer amongst them on the loose pretending to play possum. Not to mention the death of their beloved friend Christian who die in vain. In which case was the straw that broke the camel's back that something was not right. That it so happens that Will was supposed to meet them in the control room when suddenly they were knock unconscious by some sort of gas. In which they woke up from with people missing & uncounted for? Not to mention the fact that Alex Crawford literally took his last breath before collapsing in Jason's arms. From being stab in the back by the killer, as Jason told Will to explain what happen to him. That he too went missing after they woke up from being unconscious. Will just told them to meet him in the basement so that he can explain everything to them. Which seem very odd that he would lure them back to where the killer was? Which didn't seem like a very good idea? As Jason told him to meet them back in the control room where they would be waiting on him. However, Will told Jason that he must first turn on the backup generator. So, that they could see that it is him that they are talking too on the camera in the control room. It seems as if Will was true to his word & turn on the backup system. As Jason, Jill & Lisa seen Will on the camera down in the basement. In which they try to locate Christian who was still down there some where's. That judging from what transpired with the electricity it seems as if the killer didn't want them to see who was doing what? As the killer wanted to keep them in the dark about who's the one that is doing all the killing. Which was smart on the killer's part of not letting them know who is involve in this conspiracy. That from the angle of the cameras that's place in different parts of the tower. The three of them could see the six members of the Carson's family walking around the tower as if nothing happened. That somewhere within lies the killer or killers posing as an actor. Who is disguising themselves to look apart by blending in with his or her surroundings? Making things all so difficult to sort out who is working within the film as the perpetrator. Which is a reminder that this is what the anonymous person met by saying "This is where things get interesting"? Which seems to have a connection with how things have transpired so far. With the person claiming to be Eric Johnson on social media. Not to mention the craziness of how this film is turning out to be. By focusing this entire film around them as the center piece of what's to be their final cut. In solving the mystery by having them follow the signs to reveal one last detail on who else is involved in the faces of death murders case. That there is one final piece of the link that is missing from this case of Whodunnit? That there's a connection between this killer & Danny Burton & The Sandman Edgerrin James. That somehow it all traces back to the two of them & how they were able to define the odds of being undetected? That is until, someone decided to rain on their parade by spoiling their plans. Which is something that didn't set well with whoever is behind these killing. Which has the mark of death written to those who are responsible for the deaths of Danny Burton & Edgerrin James. Which means that someone is filling in on their behalf. To set the stage for one final massacre to avenge the deaths of Danny & Mr. James. For the wrongdoing of one Ms. Elizabeth Burton who was killed in a car accident by Eric & Jason along with some of their friends. According to the story Lisa has conjured up in her mind as of what is happening at this point. That the three of them are going about this thing all wrong? Considering that it's all about getting back at them for what transpired at the House of Horrors last October. Considering that it's all about getting even with the four of them for what they done. Even though, the blame was on this anonymous person who spilled the beans on the two of them. Which means that they must seek out this anonymous person before the killer does. Which is why Christian was killed due to his involvement in how it all played out at the House of Horrors that night. Considering that he was the one who killed Edgerrin James & Danny Burton. Which is starting to make sense as of why the killer than went after Jill. Considering that she was the one who help Christian killed Danny Burton. Which all seems to succumb to the logic in how the killer is formulating his or her plan. In which they all had a part to play in the demise of Danny & his partner in crime Mr. James. Which is the link that binds them all together as one whole vender in seeking some sort of retribution. Considering that Jill, Jason & Lisa wanted a little retribution of their own for the killing of their friend Christian. Which seems as if the killer & the three of them has something in common to avenge those who they have lost. It was just the matter of who would come out on top in the end? Which left the three of them with a decision on what they are planning to do? Now that they are aware of what's going on? Meanwhile, doing that time Jill found some disturbing footage of someone dress as Diane Carson killing someone in a Sam Carson costume in cold blood. Which didn't make no sense whatsoever of why the killer would go after another killer who sole purpose is to try & confuse them. On what is real & what stage as supposed to what is scripted in the movie. As they couldn't tell who was underneath those costumes. Almost as if the killer was picking off each one of the actors who was dress as one of the Carson's. Narrowing it down to see who remains in the end. Although, they would have to watch out for any signs of deception that the killer may use. As supposed to what lies waiting in the midst for them. That they too can fall victim to the killer if not careful? However, after the footage was seen the cameras begin to shut down one by one. Until all the screens begin to show static in which they lost sight of Will fort who was all alone in the basement. Jason then tries to get in touch with him by using the walkie talkie to tell him what's going on? However, in came walking in the control room was Will Fort who seem to be injured. As he told the three of them that someone try to kill him. Wearing one of the Carson costumes, as he seems conflicted on the fact that someone literally try to kill him? Jill asks Will did the killer attack him down in the basement. That they try to tell him that going down into the basement was a bad idea. However, it seems as if Will didn't have a clue about what they were talking about. That he just woke up from someone knocking him unconscious across the back of the head. The moment he turns his back on who he thought was Layla dress in Ella Carson costume. Which got the three of them thinking that if it wasn't him, they were talking too on the walkie talkie than who was it? As they could have sworn that it was him, they were talking too? That something is off about this whole ordeal. As Will begins to explain to the three of them that he was on his way down to the control room earlier to speak with them about something concerning Timothy. When suddenly he was knock out by person's unknown. Which was about ten minutes after he lost contact with them. That after all this time he regain conscious again. Which was around the time that the gas knocks them out. Which alerted Will that Elliot & Jade informed him that something was wrong & that they couldn't talk now because of the odor in the room. That he needed to stay put until they can get to him. Which is where he got knock unconscious a few minutes later by someone in a Carson getup? Which would explain where Elliot & Jade disappear too? While the four of them were knockout from the gas. Which seems too fitting that Elliot was too eager to settle the score with Will. That had them all thinking that Will & Timothy was the killers at first. Which brings up the question where in the world was Elliot & Jade as of this moment. That they need to speak with them a concerning to this matter. Even though, Jill, Jason & Lisa still didn't trust Will for that matter. Considering that his story doesn't add up either. That there is something fishy going on around here. That they were going to find Elliot & Jade no matter what? As they told Will that he is coming along with them. So, that there are no more surprises on their end? Seems as though, the three of them prepare themselves with weapons to protect themselves from whoever the killer maybe. As the rules apply to all those who are involve with this film project. Not taking any chances whatsoever being that their friend was killed on a funny style. Which makes it that much easier to assume that everyone is out to get them. Until they prove otherwise on who they can trust with their lives. While searching the tower for any signs of life. They heard a voice over the walkie talkie saying that everyone needs to report to the dayroom for a meeting. Which was perfect considering that Jill & the others would have a better understanding about what is going on?

CHAPTER 14

Whodunnit

However, when the four of them reach the dayroom, they found that the only person that show up at this point was Elliot. Who immediately went after Will for taking part in the killings of Alex & Jade? Which was a surprise to Jill & the others that the killer manages to kill again. As Elliot wanted to know what they mean by again. As Lisa explain to Elliot that the killer manages to kill their friend Christian in the process. Which was a shocker to Elliot & Will that the killer killed their friend. That's when the finger pointing begun between Will & Elliot about who's the one responsible for the killings. As they both brought up some good points about each other on the fact that Will claim that Elliot was the killer. Considering that he was the one who manage to escape the room when the gas begun to settle in. Considering that he killed Jade in the process while knocking him unconscious with the gun he is carrying around. Which was in his hand at this point. Considering that he had a score to settle with Will. Which makes total sense to Jill, Jason & Lisa who recall the fact that Elliot was supposed to meet them in the basement. Claiming to have the device that would turn on the signal so that they can call the police. As it turns out that he was a no show & that their friend was killed in the process. As Elliot denied the fact that he told them no such thing. That someone else pretending to be him told them such a thing. Considering that at the time he didn't have a walkie talkie to communicate with anyone. That by chance he mange to get a hold to one in Zorn's office. Which seems kind of suspicious to Jill, Jason, & Lisa about his story. Which brings Elliot to Will concerning his story that he was the one who killed Alex Crawford who must have known something about what was going on & came to warn them. That after all he

& Timothy was the ones who everyone suspects as being the killers in the first place. That he was the one who shot & killed Timothy to protect Jill & Lisa from being killed. Which again brings up the fact that it was Will who they talk too on the walkie talkie. Who suggested that it was all for show that Elliot killed Timothy? As Elliot also mention that it was him who attack them in the control room after the killing of Alex Crawford. Until he begins to ring out shots from the gun which is probably how he got injured. Claiming that he was attack from behind. That for all he knows Will probably fake the whole thing in order to remain hidden. That the three of them are going by what he says. That Jill, Jason & Lisa must remember that the killer loves to play mind games. By using any & everything to try & confuse them as of who to believe. As both of their stories seems to have great points about who is doing what? When the whole time the three of them was thinking that maybe they both was in on it together. Considering that the killer would love for them to drop their guard when face with adversity. Which makes things difficult to sort out as of why things are the way they are? Of not being able to understand the meaning of it all. Considering that someone is trying to mess with their minds. By causing all sorts of conflict with the killings of other supposedly killers which would determine how the script is to be the decisive factor. Which the real killer is using to complicate things by turning the script into a real-life scenario. Which makes it hard for the three of them to tell who is telling the truth & who is lying to them. Which put the three of them in an awkward position. As they decided to stick with one another & not to trust anyone. As Jason warn Will & Elliot to back off & to not come any closer to them. As he told them both that they were going to leave & to not follow them or else there will be hell to pay. As they both tries to plead their case that one is trying to frame the other. In which Jason, Jill & Lisa wasn't trying to hear as the lights shut off once again. Leaving them all to defend for themselves while the killer lurks within the dark room. As Jason grab Lisa & Jill's hand to get away from the two of them. While retreating they could hear one of them scream out for help. Although, they couldn't tell who it was be killed in the process. All they were concern with was to get as far away from as they could from the commotion. However, after the disturbance they could hear someone, footsteps coming toward them from behind. Almost as if someone was following them as they ran through the tower. While in a panic state of mind of not knowing what to do. That if push comes to shove, they will have to take a stand against whoever

is following them. As the three of them begun to stand their ground to defend themselves if need be. In came running toward them with a flashlight yelling to the three of them to help them. Was someone they thought they never see which was Laura & Seth Myers who were sort of missing in action ever since the killings begun to take place. As Jill, Jason & Lisa wanted to know where the two of them been hiding. That suddenly, they appear out of no where's. Claiming to that someone lock them in one of the hidden compartments in the tower. Who was all cover up in blood, as the two of them wanted to know what was going on? That while they were confined to the hidden room. They begin to smell a funny odor coming from the air vents. Next thing they know they were out of it? However, when they woke up, they found themselves in another room with three dead bodies. Two of them were crew members from the film the other one was dressed in one of the Carson's attires. That being Ella Carson costume who seem dead as a doornail. That person being Layla Martinez who played the part of Ella Carson. Which is how they discover that someone try to frame them by covering them up in blood while holding a knife. Which seems pretty far-fetch to Jill & the others as they wanted to see for themselves the bodies Laura & Seth claim to have seen. Even though, they still have their doubts about the two of them concerning the matter. As Laura & Seth showed Jill, Jason & Lisa the room where they saw the three dead bodies. However, when it came time to show them the proof that they weren't trying to deceive them. The joke was on the three of them as there were no sign of dead bodies any where's to be found. That it seems all too familiar that the two of them appear right after leaving Will & Elliot behind. Not soon after they would hear one of them scream if not both. Who showed up in blood not soon afterwards to meet with them? Which seems sort of odd of why the two of them came after the three of them. After paying a visit to Will & Elliot who was unaware of their presence. Which had the three of them wondering was it the two of them. Who suggested that they meet up in the dayroom? Which was a diversion to get everyone into one room so that they could killed two birds with one stone. However, they didn't count on the three of them sticking together through it all. Which the two of them had to come up with something else to cover up what they did. However, Laura & Seth denied the fact that they had anything to do with the murder of Will Fort. As they got the same message on the walkie talkie to meet in the dayroom for a meeting. That by the time they reach them the lights had shut off & then they heard someone scream which was Will. Who they spotted lying on the floor with a knife stuck in his back? With a note attached to it that read Whodunnit. That according to the three of them the only other person down there with them was Elliot. Who they didn't see no where's around? Which begs the question where he stands in all this controversy. That the same could be said about him as of how well they know him. Considering that he is a very private about his life. Which is something Jill, Jason & Lisa must take in consideration as they figure it to be the case about each one of them. Who is running the show behind the scenes of this film? That because of it, their friend was made to suffer the consequences for their actions. Which begs the question of Whodunnit? Which is something the three of them are determined to find out. Which bring up the question about Layla who obviously loves to play mind games at their expense. As the question now is if she is in on it. That from the start her behavior toward them had been under suspicion from the beginning. That she just may be the one behind it all? However, the jury is still out on who's the one responsible for all of this. That they must consider the fact that just because Laura & Seth said that Will is dead. Doesn't mean that the three of them are going to take their word for it. Considering that their word doesn't mean a thing. Considering that they could be full of it as well. Not to mention the fact that the two of them still couldn't explain what happened to the three supposedly dead bodies that they saw. Then again there's that chance they could be telling the truth considering that Elliot may have played a factor in Will's death. Although, they could have staged the whole thing to make it seems as if the two of them were innocent. Although, there's a good chance that Layla may have killed Will. In which case it seems to the three of them that they are on the end of a double-edged sword. On whom the perpetrator is? Although, there was one thing that the three of them couldn't figure out. Is which one of them is playing possum by disguising their voice in order to conceal their identity. Meanwhile, Jill, Jason & Lisa heard the voice of Christian on the walkie talkie. As he sounded awful almost as if he was dying sort of speech. Which brought hope in the eyes of his friends to come & help him. That he is still down in the basement waiting on them.

CHAPTER 15

Sixth Sense

Words doesn't begin to express how appreciative the three of them seem to hear Christian's voice. Almost as if a weight has been lifted off their chest. As now wasn't the time to figure out who done what, when their friend needs some medical assistance. They all rush down to the basement to see where Christian is. While Laura went to go see if she can find a first aid kit in the control room. Not wanting her to go alone Seth volunteer to go with her to assist with finding a first aid kit to help Christian. In order to prove to Jason, Lisa & Jill that they are here to help. Which sounds like a plan to Jason & the others who went to go look for their friend. While Laura & Seth went to go see about seeking some assistance for Christian. However, once the three of them got down there. They seem to be very alert about their surroundings. Not knowing if the killer is still down there lurking around waiting for the perfect opportunity to strike. Which didn't matter to them, that all they wanted to do is to find their friend at this point. Considering there's a good chance that they could save him if he just holds on a little longer. It seems as if the three of them was having a bit of trouble trying to locate him. As they try calling out to him on the walkie talkie & in the basement. However, there wasn't any responds back from Christian. As they figure that maybe he lost conscious or that maybe they arrive a little too late. However, Lisa felt as if something wasn't right about this whole thing. Almost as if she has a sixth sense about the whole ordeal. That maybe it wasn't Christian who they were talking too on the walkie talkie. That yes" it sounded like him, but what if it wasn't him? Which seem impossible to Jason as there was no way that was someone else. Speaking on the behalf of Christian considering that how is that possible. As Jill begin to agree with Lisa that *something just feels off? Almost as if someone is trying to deliberately deceive them by using Christian's voice. That maybe the killer is using Christian to lure them into a trap. Which didn't make no sense considering that Christian would rather die than to put them in any danger. Figuring that maybe Christian is in trouble the three of them begin to hear someone screaming out in pain as if they were being torture by the killer. Although, they couldn't tell where the screaming was coming from? Seems as though, it was coming from all sides of the basement. As they figure it to be Christian who was the one being torture. As they all begin to call out for Christian to see where he was. However, it seems as if the screams were getting worse as the three of them constantly call out for him. In which case Lisa & Jill couldn't bear any longer as the two of them begin to whimper softly. As they all felt helpless to try & help their friend in his time of need. Considering that Christian is made to suffer the consequences for not complying with the killer's demand. In order to get to his friends Jill, Lisa & Jason. Which proves that Christian is sacrificing himself in order to save the three of them. However, it wasn't very wise that Jason begins to lose his cool. As he just went off by calling out the killer to pick on someone their own size. That he is willing to take on whoever the killer maybe. As he calls out the killer to come for him that he's the one the killer is after? As Jason told Jill & Lisa to prepare themselves for what maybe the fight of their lives. As the three of them prepare themselves for battle with the killer with the weapons they had. Then suddenly the screaming stop & they begin to hear silence once again. It seems as if the three of them was ready to go to war with the killer. As they begin to hear footsteps coming toward them. Although, it was hard to tell who or where the footsteps were coming from? Considering that it was dark down in the basement & that it was hard to pin point where the footsteps was coming from. Since they had arm themselves with weapons to avoid being ambush by the killer. Even though they had one flashlight between them to see what was going on around them. It was then that they spotted Seth Myers stumbling toward them yelling to them to help him. It wasn't until he fell that they realize that he's been stab multiple times in the back by the killer. Who had a knife stuck in his back with a note saying Whodunnit? It was then that they all came rushing to his aid. To see if they can assist him in any way possible with his injuries. As Lisa & the others wanted to know where was Laura that if she too had been killed by the killer? Seth told the three of them that he doesn't know if Laura is okay or not. That he was caught off guard by the killer who surprise him. When his back was turned? However, before they could ask him another important question? Like where was Laura when this happened? It seems as if the poor guy had passed away from his injuries. Which had them all wondering if Laura had something to do with his death. That maybe it was him who they heard screaming in pain. Then just as things couldn't get any obvious for the three of them to sort out. In came into the picture was Laura screaming that the killer is right behind her. Which alerted Jill, Lisa & Jason to grab their weapons to begin the assault on the killer who is right behind Laura. However, when it came time for the killer to appear. It seems as if no one was there behind her who she claims was chasing her. That suddenly, this so-called killer happens to come after her. The moment Seth gets stab in the back by the same killer who so happens to be behind him. When suddenly she appears moments after this occurred? As Seth made it very clear that the attack occurs while his back was turned. Which leaves only one possibility that she is to blame for his death? That they also notice that she doesn't' have a scratch on her any where's to be found. Which seems sort of bizarre that she doesn't have not one scratch on her. Claiming that she's been attack by the killer who was supposedly after her. Which seems suspicious of how she manages to escape with her life. As Jill, Jason & Lisa didn't feel comfortable around her. Considering that her story doesn't add up about what she claims has happened. As Jill suggested that Laura go on her separate way. Away from the three of them considering that she is not to be trusted. However, Laura insisted that she is not the killer that she is afraid to be alone. That if they are going to make it through than they all need to stick together to make sure no one else dies. That Laura is willing to go as far as to help them find the person responsible for the killings. That if they want to, they can tie her hands up to ensure that she doesn't do anything out of the ordinary. In order to prove to them that she is not who they think she is? Which seems like a done deal to the three of them that she can be some use to them. Considering that she is Zorn's assistant which means she has everything to do with this? Which means that she has the insight on everyone involve in this film. Considering that she is the one who can shed some light on who is behind these killings. By helping them search each person background from top to bottom. That may have a connection with the four of them regarding their past. Although Christian was a non-factor at this moment. Considering now that it's just the three of them who is left with a decision to come to a crossroad regarding their past lives. That someone from the past is trying to get their attention by setting the stage for what is to be the final call. That if memory serves them correctly then things are going to get a lot more interesting from this moment on. According to what they experience throughout history when it comes to this sort of thing. Considering that they are in for a big surprise judging from the clues they have gotten. Like the person declaring to be Eric Johnson which could be where things get interesting according to this anonymous person. Who told Jill to beware the bucket list, in result to the fear of death? Which means that whoever this person is. Wanted to make themselves known that things are going to get a lot more interesting for the four of them. Considering that one of them is down for the count & that three more remain to be executed by the executioner. Whose sole purpose is to set straight the narrative by righting the wrongs for the wrongdoing of the past. Which means that they all are marked for death, especially for Jill, Jason & Lisa who remain the target. However, Lisa insisted that they can catch whoever it may be behind these killings with the help of Laura. Before the killer decides to strike again which will also give them the upper hand on who is the person behind the scenes that is causing all this chaos. By revealing the killer's identity before he or she can get to them. By doing a little bit of digging on each person background check to see who is the personator behind it all? As Laura mention to the three of them that Zorn has a secret room in the tower that he uses to oversee everything in the film. Which is where he creates the magic that only she knows about. Considering that this is where he keeps all his information at? Considering that there's a strong possible he maybe in that room hiding there until the coast is clear. In which Jason & the others wanted Laura to show them this secret room that Zorn has hidden away in the tower. However, they would be interrupted by a disturbing call they receive on the walkie talkie. From someone claiming to be Layla who seems to be in distress at that present time. Who seem to be in some sort of trouble & needed some assistance from anyone who is listening to her cries for help?*

CHAPTER 16

The Endgame

That judging from the sound of her voice it seems as if she was in a world of trouble. As Laura ask Layla where in the tower is she located, so that they can help her. The poor girl seems out of it as to where she is. So, Laura suggested that Layla meet them at the secret location where they have their meeting at? Which was a room Jill & her friends knew nothing about. As Laura told the three of them not to worry because there's a secret room in the tower that only a few people know about. That Layla is one of the few people who knows of this room along with a few crew members. As Layla agree to meet them at the spot. However, there were a few speculations on the part of Jill & her two friends. That Layla isn't to be trusted considering that this could be one of her games. By setting the three of them up for another one of her mind games which is loves to play. That there's a strong possibility that she is the killer. Although, they weren't sure it was even her they were talking too? That the killer has a way to disguise his or her voice to make it seem as if they were talking to someone else. Just like the killer did with Christian who they thought was alive. However, it seems as if the killer manages to somehow record his voice & use it to lure them into a trap. That if its really Layla than they will have to take certain precaution to not fall into another one of the killer sneaks' attacks. That this time around they are going to be better prepare for what the killer has in store for them. That they are not going to fall for the same trick twice. As Jason told Laura to tell Layla to make herself known when they meet her at the spot. That they don't want anymore surprises from her. That now? Is not the time for her foolish games. However, it seems as if they got no responds from Layla who was probably in a predicament where is couldn't speak. Considering that she did mention that she is in some sort of trouble. However, she didn't say what kind of trouble she is in, as Layla fail to mention that part to them. Which makes it even more the reason to take precaution. Not knowing what may occur when expecting the unexpected to happened? Which is something the three of them pick up on. Considering what they went through in the past that has the same reference to it. That they must beware of anything unusual that may involve some repercussion along the way. While making their way to the secret room. Jill & her friends seems surprised how well Laura knew her way through the tower. Almost as if she was taking them on a tour of the place. Of all the hidden compartments that was lay out in this structure of a place. That no wonder how the killer was able to maneuver around without being notices. That it takes an expert to know every inch of this building by hand. Which got the three of them thinking that the killer is someone who knows the in & out of this place. That according to Laura very few people knew about the secrets to this place. Which got them thinking once again about Zorn who is the mastermind behind it all. That somehow, he is connected to what's happening. Considering that it was him who wanted them in the first place to be in his film. A film that hits so close to home. As they try to understand what his involvement was in all this chaos. However, when they reach the hidden room where there were all sorts of controls that were fixated on how the tower was run. As far as the sound effects go's which would explain where the sounds were coming from? Meanwhile, Laura tries desperately to get in touch with Layla to see if she has made it to the room. What they would hear from the other end of the walkie talkie was out of the ordinary. As they heard a whisper saying to them" Over Here"? Which seems very odd as of who it was that was calling them. As they couldn't make out where this person was hiding at? Considering that it was dark & that the only thing they had was a flashlight to see what was around them. That telling them" Over Here" didn't help the situation all that much. As the four of them tries to figure out where over here is. As they suddenly heard a ruckus coming from behind them that instantly cause them to turn around to see who it was behind them. As Laura thought that it was Layla playing her games again. However, when Jason flashes the light toward where the commotion was. They all seen that someone had knock something heavy over. At that point, they all begin to get nervous about who is in the room with them. That as of now, it seems as if the killer has drag them into another situation where they had to arm themselves with weapons. In order to defend themselves from what seems to be another sneak attack. As the voice continue to say" Over Here"? Only this time it seems as if the whisper was coming from some where's in the room. As Jason & the others tries to locate where the whispering was coming from in the room. It would seem as if they all had gotten the surprise of a lifetime when out of no where's appear Elliot. Who manages to scare them all by the sudden appearance? In which they were not expecting to happen? As they all wanted to know where Layla was considering that she was supposed to meet them here. Elliot told them that he doesn't know where Layla is. That if she is still alive than there's a possibility, she may be the one responsible for what is going on here. That according to him there's that chance that she may have fake her own death. In order to carry out whatever her plans are to bring attention to this film. By recreating the scenes from this movie in order to create movie magic. By taking it a step further by creating an environment basic on a real-life scenario. Which will bring revenue to the entertainment business. As of how the killer manages to escape at the end of this film. Which would shed some light around the fact that there is a copycat killer on the loose. That the blame would go toward Zorn as the one who killed everyone including Jill & her friends. In order to get rating for capturing his so-called movie magic by creating turmoil within the movie. Who eventually kills himself in the end to put a bit of a spin to it? As the final resolution to the faces of death murder case. Which seems to be Layla's plan in order to cover her tracks by putting the blame on Zorn. While she gets all the exposure as being the only survivor on set. Which is the assumption Elliot came up with as a possibility of what is going on. In which case Jill & the others couldn't disagree with. According to the behavior she has shown Jill & her other comrades. That it was no secret that she has it in for them by the way she constantly made it clear that she is willing to do anything to make their lives miserable. That she even went as far as to resurrect the faces of death masks to get her point across. By marking them & everyone else for death. Which put things in perspective according to the detail as of how things transpire within reasoning. That the truth is finally starting to become clear as of who the perpetrator is? Although, Jill, Jason & Lisa still had their doubts about who else maybe involve. Considering that they can't be too sure about what the perception maybe. Of what may come off as a deception of what is reality. According to what was reference in the past that appearance can indeed be deceiving. That the three of them still has their work cut out for them as of who is to blame for all this chaos. That the truth may lies within the links of the chain that seems to have a connection between Danny & Mr. James & this killer. Which is something the three of them believe very dearly. That there is no doubt that this has something to do with the past. Although, they had a very hard time trying to soak in everything that has been stored upon them. Which is something they couldn't put their finger on as of who to believe at this point. That the jury is still out on that theory that is until they discover someone lying slouch down in a chair. Dress in a Ben Carson costume who seems to be passed out or as if seems. That whoever it maybe could be playing possum like before when the same thing happens to their friend Christian. In which case Jill, Jason & Lisa wasn't taking any chance by going near whoever it maybe. So, Elliot decided to go play the hero by putting himself in harm way. By checking to see if the person underneath the Ben Carson costume is actual dead or playing possum. Intense feel the air as Elliot got closer to the body. Which is where he discovers that whoever it was? Is dead as a doornail. In which case there was no way of telling how this individual was killed. However, when Elliot removed the mask from this person's face. They discover that the individual was non other than Zorn who seems as if he was strangle to death by the killer. Who made it his or her priority to make a statement? By stating the obvious that there's indeed a killer amongst them. Which seems to be where they all the commotion was coming from when they heard a noise coming from that same area a moment ago. Before Elliot momentarily arrives on the scene. Which seems suspicious of what length the killer will go. In order to create chaos & confusion within the surroundings of who is the perpetrator that is playing mind games with the three of them. That perhaps Laura & Elliot could be the one's who are partially responsible for what is going on here. That there is that chance the two of them could be the killers. Who are faking this whole thing by playing innocent the whole time? When the two of them are trying to lure the three of them into a situation that is hard to get out of. That the only way they can be sure is to come up with a plan to separate the two of them. So, that they can get down to business to check their background history.

CHAPTER 17

The Perpetrator

Although, it would be risky if they decide to not proceed with their investigation. Considering that the two of them are working together which could be the case or not. Considering that the three of them didn't want to play their hand. Until they know for sure who the killer is. That they are going to continue with the course of action to not let Laura or Elliot know what they are up too. That the plan is to let things run its course for now. That when the moment comes to seize the opportunity Jill, Jason & Lisa will be ready. Considering that the three of them didn't want to alarm Laura & Elliot that they are on to them. Considering that they both seem suspicious when it comes down to who killed Seth & Will Fort. That that both was alone with each one of them when they were killed. Then again there's that chance what Elliot had mention before about Layla being the killer could prove to be relevant. As the push continues to search for Christian's killer. Which reminded Jason to ask Laura did she know where they can find the device that Zorn use to turn off the signal for the cellphones. Which she knew right off hand where it was located & offer to take them there. However, Lisa mentioned to Laura that she has other things to attend too. Like helping them find the killer like she promises. As Lisa sort hinted to remind her about the background checks. Which seems as if they ran into a little situation on the issue considering that Laura was the only one beside Zorn who knew where the device was located. Which didn't seem like a big deal considering that Jason offers to go find it. If Laura could direct him & Elliot to the area where it is located at? Which is how they were going to separate the two of them just in case something jumps off. Which is perfect considering that if it is the two of them that is pulling the strings behind the scenes. That by splitting up the group is their main priority to get each of them alone. Which is something the three of them are counting on to happened. That being Jason all alone with Elliot while Jill & Lisa are alone with Laura. Keeping a close eye on things that is going on between the two of them. By communicating with one another through the walkie talkie. Which Laura will use to guide Jason & Elliot to the spot where the device is held at? While also using the computer to search each person's background. However, in order to do that she must first turn on the emergency back up system. Which was established for that room only. Just in case of an emergency like now. However, Elliot was unaware of what was going on considering what Laura is planning to do once him & Jason leaves the room. Considering that they didn't want him knowing that they are going to run a background check on him along with everyone else. Now that the plan is in place of finally sort this thing out. It seems as if Jason & Elliot was on their way to find the device. As Laura begins to guide them through the tower to the place where the device is located. While at the same time searching the background of each employee that is associated with this film project. It seems as if everything checks out good with most of them. However, there was one individual that stood out from the rest. As this person's background seem shocking to the three of them about what was mentioned in this person's history. Which is a major discovery on who is behind the killings. That this person whole demeanor was nothing more than a lie to begin with. That had everyone fool from the start as of who this person really was? Which brought their attention to Jason who was unaware of the danger that lurks within his surroundings. Considering that they must be very careful not to alert the killer by any means necessary. Of putting their friend Jason in any kind of danger. However, the plan was to wait until the perfect time to tell Jason the truth when the coast is clear. Considering that there is a killer amongst him who is bearing down on him. As Lisa told Jason that he needs to be very careful considering that he is in danger. However, Jill & Lisa wanted to know where was Elliot at the time. As they wanted to know was, he nearby. Jason told them that he is right behind him. In the meantime, it seems as if Jason & Elliot arrive at their destination with the help of Laura. The only problem is trying to find the device in the dark. In which Jason told Elliot that they should split up to find the device. Which was the opportunity Jill, Lisa & Laura was looking for the get Jason alone so that they could tell him what is going on. Jason then begins to ask them did they find out anything on each one *of the casts & crew background. Jill told him that everyone checks out alright except for one. That person being none other than Elliot Smith whose real name is Eli James the son of Edgerrin James aka The Sandman. However, before Jason could react to the news, he was hit from behind by Eli James with the gun he was carrying around. Knocking Jason unconscious while he searches for the device. In which the walkie talkie went on dead silence. As Jill tries desperately to get in touch with Jason to see why he is not responding to her calls. Which means only one thing is that Eli must have gotten a hold to him. In which Jill & Lisa wasn't going to stand for. Of having to lose another one of their friends in the process. As Jill & Lisa wanted Laura to show them where Jason was to see if he was okay. However, Laura insisted that they stay while she goes & look for Jason & the device. Considering that the two of them are better off where they are? Considering that Eli is after the two of them now that it is down to them both. Considering that now he will be coming after them & not her which means that if she can find the device before Eli does? She can call for help in time before he gets the chance to get to them. That they must consider that they are in a safe place as of now considering that they have light to see if he tries to enter this room. That they can better prepare themselves for what's to come. Instead of entering the dark tower with her to find the device. That she knows where the device is hidden & he doesn't. That she purposely didn't tell Jason where it was? Considering that Eli was just waiting for the opportunity to present itself. To take the device right from underneath Jason noise. Which is something he knew the three of them would come looking for? In which his plan would come into full play of finishing what his father started. Which makes all the sense in the world of how he is link to all the murders that has occur. That he was the one who shot & killed Timothy Jones. Not to mention the that he was the one who was with Will & Jade when they allegedly were killed while in his presents. That he is the perpetrator who use the Carson Family costumes worn by the cast in order to try & frame them. Just as he tries to do with Layla only the story ends with him trying to get away with it, instead of Layla. Which is what he wanted everyone to believe by setting up a false narrative. So, that he can get away with it, just as his father tries to do. As the saying goes like father, like son. That he's the one responsible for killing Christian in a fit of rage. That was once share by his father & Danny Burton who would stop at nothing until they seek justices for the murder of his fiancé. Only this time around Eli was seeking justices for his father who was killed at the House of Horror at last year's festivities. That now he is on a mission to get even with the people who killed his father. However, that wasn't going to stop Jill & Lisa from foiling his plans by seeking retribution for Christian & Jason who has suffer in the process. As the two of them came to a decision that they are not going to be a victim anymore. That they are going to put an end to it once & for all. Meanwhile, Laura went to go get the device & check on Jason to see if he is still alive. As Laura promise to give them an update on his condition once she finds him. While Lisa & Jill stay put until they get word that everything is okay from Laura. In the meanwhile, Jill & Lisa was planning what's their next move once Laura gives them the signal that everything is okay. However, nothing would prepare them for what would happen next. As the two of them have gotten an unexpected call from Elliot on the walkie talkie. Who told them that they would be next on the killer's list? By giving them a final warning that they need to beware the bucket list, in result to the fear of death. In which case Jill didn't understand at first, but now she is beginning to realize what the killer meant by those words. That for once she understood the point Eli was trying to make when he refers the four of them to the bucket list. That he would eventually cross off his list by killing each one of them. That would result in being tormented by the mark of the beast. Which is the curse of the Faces of Death method. Which is the blueprint for seek out one's retaliation for someone else's wrongdoing? That soon they will be face with the truth of what stands before them. That there no getting out of this situation that calls for them all to be sentence to death? As Eli left them with these words to abide by, is that death is coming for them both. That they should prepare themselves for the surprise of a lifetime to unfold right before their eyes. As he pointed out that they aren't going to see this coming. At that point, Jill & Lisa heard nothing further as they try to get Eli to tell them what he did with Jason. However, they wouldn't get a respond from him, seems as though he turns off the walkie talkie. Which they begin to worry that something bad must have happened to Jason. As Jill couldn't wait any longer for Laura's responds on Jason's condition.*

CHAPTER 18

The Big Reveal

So, they decided to come up with a plan that would benefit their wellbeing. By not waiting around for something to happen, when they could take matters into their own hands. Considering that they just may come in handy if Laura needs some sort of assistance. That they aren't going to sit around when there is so much at stake. Considering that their lives depend on how things would turn out. That it is up to the two of them to put the final nail in the coffin. So, instead of waiting for Eli James to come to them. They decided to go face him head on to end this thing once & for all. Considering that he had cause enough damage already. That it is up to them to put a stop to it by facing their fears. While searching for the tower for Laura to see if she has come up on the device & to see if Jason was alright. Although, it seems as if they weren't getting any responds back from Laura on the walkie talkie. Which could mean one or two things is that one is has been killed by Eli or that they both are in on it together. Considering that there no telling what surprises awaits them. That for all they know this could have been part of their plan from the get-go. That there's no telling what Eli & Laura are up too. That Jill & Lisa must take in consideration that the two of them are working together. Then suddenly they heard Laura on the walkie talkie screaming bloody murder. As if she was being attack by Eli James the killer who may have caught up with her. Without wasting anytime on the subject Laura yell out to Jill & Lisa that she has turn on the device. Which was all she could say before the two-way radio cut out. At that point Jill & Lisa both took out their cellphones to call the authorities. When suddenly they got a call back from Laura on the walkie talkie to tell the two of them to meet her down in the dayroom. Because she has found Jason alive & that they were on their way down to the dayroom. Which brought up the question was it really her who was screaming a moment ago. Laura told them that she was under attack by Eli James when suddenly Jason came to her rescue. Which made perfect sense to them, as they told Laura that they are on the way down to meet with them. However, on their way down to the dayroom it seems as if Lisa had become distracted by something. Which brought her attention else where's while Jill continues to the dayroom without her. It wasn't until she reaches the dayroom that Jill discovers that Lisa is missing. She then begins to call out for her to see where she may have wander off too but got no responds back. Which means that Eli must have gotten a hold to her, while she wasn't looking. Jill then begins to call out for Laura & Jason to see if they had made it down there to her. Still there wasn't any answer from either one of them. So, Jill decided to call the police instead, to get some assistance from them. However, that call would be interrupted by Eli James who demanded that she ends the call or else. Who suddenly appear out of no where's with the gun he was carrying around? Who pointed it straight at Jill who were minutes away from calling the police? Jill tries to reason with him, but Eli wasn't trying to hear what she has to say at this point. As she demanded to know what he did with Lisa, Jason & Laura. Although, he reframes from answering any of her questions & just demanded that she hands over the cellphone to him. However, Jill seems reluctant to hand over her phone without some sort of explanation about the whereabouts of her friends. Which made Eli cock back the handle of the gun. To show that he wasn't playing around. Which Jill seem to oblige by handing over her cellphone to him. Once she spotted someone dress in the Ella Carson costume who seems to be making a move toward Eli from behind him. In which case this person seems to be working together with Jill to bring Eli down to for the count. As Jill kept Eli James busy by distracting him. While the person in the Ella Carson costume sneaks up behind him to deliver the final blow. In which they exceed in doing by catching him off guard by the sudden blow that rendered him helpless. In which case Jill couldn't thank the person in the Ella Carson costume enough for saving her life. As she thought that someone was one of her friends coming to her aid. As she then grabs the cellphone & begin to call the police once again with her back turned to this person in the Ella Carson costume. When suddenly the person in the Ella Carson costume bent down to pick up the gun Eli had in his hand. To only use it to knock Jill over the head with, considering the sudden twist of turn of *events. That allows this person to deceive Jill in thinking that they were there to help her out. When suddenly she was betrayed by this individual who saw the chance to manipulate her. By taking advantage of her vulnerability when she least expected. As this individual begins to set the stage for the big reveal of finally answering the million-dollar question. It seems as if everything is a go to start the third & final act to this conspiracy of a conclusion of a story. As everything seems to be in place to start the show of who's behind the murder mystery of this film. As the person in the Ella Carson costume started by waking up Jill with some sort of smelling salts which instantly had an effect. On how Jill came too of having to feel sort of confuse about why she is restrained to a chair by this individual who help her bring down the killer Eli James. Follow by two others who also was restrained to a chair with bags over their heads. Along side Eli James who was laid out on the floor from the blow he endures from this individual. That judging from the laid out of this situation doesn't seems fitting in any way possible for her. Of escaping this person's conviction toward her. Considering that whoever is in the Ella Carson costume knows about Jill & her friends. That this person was no stranger to what has happened throughout the years of their story. Concerning the background of each event what has taken place with the killers Danny Burton & Edgerrin James. That got Jill thinking that whoever it is behind the Ella Carson costume. Has also been there throughout those killings that took place years back with Danny & The Sandman James. That whoever it maybe knows the history behind those killings that had to deal with the two killers Danny Burton & Edgerrin James. That somehow involves his son Eli James which is something Jill can't understand of how he is involved in all this chaos. That he too suffers the same faith as her with the person dress in the Ella Carson costume knocking them both unconscious for the time being. As Jill was dying to know just who this person was that is causing all this chaos on set. That there was no denying the fact that whoever it maybe is directing all their intentions toward her. That she is the cause for all of this? Which the person in the Ella Carson costume expresses to Jill in a very angry way. Of how this person waited so long for this opportunity to present itself. To where this person could avenge her loved one. By getting payback to inflicted as much pain to her loved ones as possible. So, that she knows how this person feels every day. Which was something Jill couldn't bring herself to understand of what she did so badly that would have this person so angry with her. Considering that the killers got what they deserve.*

However, there was one killer who didn't deserve what happened to him. According to this person who seem very passionate about whoever this other killer is. Considering that this person warns Jill to beware the bucket list, in which it will result to the fear of death. Just as this person promises. In which case seems to be the predicament Jill is now in. However, the talk was now over & now its time for Jill to reap what she sows as the person begins to remove the mask of Ella Carson. To reveal this person's identity of who is the one behind these murders as of late. It seems as if the dead has risen from the grave when the identity of this person was revealed to Jill. As she couldn't believe what she was seeing. That to her surprise the killer this time around was none other than Rochelle Mitchell. Her roommate bestie from college who was consider dead at the House of Horrors. Who was allegedly killed by one of the killers at that time? However, it seems as if the whole thing was stage to make it seems as if she was killed by one of them. Which she so happens to mention to Jill as a doubletake to deceive her & the others. From the perception of reality for her plan to work. Which got Jill thinking what plan Rochelle is referring too. Rochelle told her that she will reveal the plan to her later, but first it was time to play a little game called. Who's underneath the two bags that is going to change the course of this entire situation. That these two individuals are the enter piece behind this entire investigation. As of what role these two individuals play along with her in resolving this issue concerning her loved one. As she begins by pulling the bag from person number one. Which was Jason her alleged boyfriend who is at fault as much as her. Who seems unaware about what is going on? With how things unfolded with the surprising appearance of Jill's friend Rochelle who they all thought was dead. However, that wasn't the end of the surprise as there was one more surprise left. As Rochelle move over to the next person who had the bag over their face. As Rochelle told them both that they are not going to believe who she manages to run into while planning her next move. That this person is the key to all that has happened in the past involving the two killers Danny Burton & Edgerrin James.

CHAPTER 19

Shedding Some Light on the Truth

Considering that the missing pieces to the puzzle are now going to unfold. When the links to the chain starts to connect once again to establish the whole truth behind the story that follows the Faces of Death murders case. By shedding some light on the truth of what really went down the night of Elizabeth Burton murder. Which catch the attention of Jill & Jason who seem interested in what Rochelle has to say about that night. However, before getting into the story there was someone who Rochelle wanted Jill & Jason to meet. Which was the person underneath the bag who was the key player to how things would play out from that night until now. As Rochelle introduce Jill & Jason to the person who witness the turn of events that took place that night. That involved the hit & run situation with one Elizabeth Burton who was struck by Eric Johnson's car. That person being none other than Grady O'Malley a drunken individual who go under the nickname Old Drunken O'Malley. Who happened to witness everything that took place that night? Which involved Rochelle's stepbrother Eric Johnson. As Jill & Jason immediately starts to connect the dots. As of who was the one claiming to be Eric Johnson that was sending Jill all those nasty comments over the death of Eric Johnson. As Rochelle mention before in the House of Horrors that there's a killer amongst them. Which so happens to be Jill as she was the one who killed her stepbrother in a suit of rage. All because she thought that he was the killer. When clearly, he met her no harm & was just trying to help them solve the mystery. That the quote was met for Jill & not Jason who they all thought the two killers Danny & The Sandman was referring too. As of being the killer amongst them that brought Rochelle to the story about that night

Elizabeth Burton was killed. That there were a few things Danny & Edgerrin James fail to mention in that story about what really happened that night. Like how at the ceremony before the day of their wedding. Elizabeth Burton had a few too many who insisted on driving home that night without a chauffeur. Which ended up with her falling asleep at the wheel which was the reason why she wrecks her car. Then had the nerve to call her soon to be husband who was a police officer at the time to come bail her out of the situation. Knowing good & well that she had no business driving in the predicament she was in? In which Rochelle put some of the blame on Danny & Edgerrin James who should of offer to drive her home that night. Knowing that she wasn't fit to drive that night. However, Danny Burton & Edgerrin James agrees to meet up with her. So, that she won't get in trouble by the law. Which is where he comes in to save her from all that trouble. However, it seems as if Elizabeth was still under the influence as she seen a car approaching & assume that it was her son & her fiancé coming to her rescue. As she then stumbles out into the road to flag down the driver who she thought was her family. When she was hit by Eric's car who he tries to avoid at all costs, but because of her stupidity her brother was now caught in the middle of this mess. That according to O'Malley's story what happen next was poor judgement on the parts of Danny & Edgerrin James. Who seem upset that Elizabeth Burton was no longer alive & reluctant to avenge her death by getting even with Eric, Jason & a couple of their friends? Although, they try to cover up the fact that Elizabeth was drunk & that they didn't want the department to find out about her. As they demanded that Grady help them bury Elizabeth body down in the woods in a secret location where no one would look. As they then threaten him that if he mentions any of this to anyone. Then there would be consequences for his action. Considering that no one is going to believe a drunk any way who can't even get through the day without a drink. As everyone took him to be a joke anyhow by how he carries himself. That even if he did say something to the authorities about what happen. Who would they rather believe a drunk or one of their own? Which gave him even more reason to drink knowing that he plays apart in the cover up. However, the last straw for Grady was when her brother was killed along with several other teenagers. Who were innocent that had nothing to do with the decision of one Elizabeth Burton who was the cause of her own murder? As Rochelle then ask the question who is really at fault for all of this? As she pointed the gun toward

O'Malley who she partially blames for her brother's murder. Considering that he waited until the last minute to mention it to her about what really happened the night of the accident. After her brother was killed by Jill. However, it seems as if the two of them came up with a plan to get even with Danny Burton & Edgerrin James for all of what they done. That the plan was already in place that all she needed to do is to intervene by being a part of Danny & Mr. James plan. Considering that they needed a third party to take the fall after they killed Jason & his friends at the House of Horrors. Which is where she comes in as a participant to take part in the scheme. As Edgerrin James promises her that she would be well off with the money she would receive for doing this? Although she already knew that it was a bunch of B's that there wasn't any money involved. That because of Grady she knew their true intention which involved the killings of her & O'Malley considering that they didn't want to leave any stones unturned. That would lead back to the two of them getting away with murdering several people including Jason & his friends. It was so obvious that the two of them were so wrap up in how they were going to get away with it. That they didn't realize that she & O'Malley was setting them up for failure. As Rochelle took it upon herself to give Jill & her two buddies the upper hand by spilling the beans on who Danny & Edgerrin James were. That she was the anonymous person who spill the beans on them. That it was because of her that the mix up happened between Jill & Danny Burton when Jill & Jason both thought that the person in the Michael Myers mask was Danny Burton. When Christian pulls off the Michael Myers mask the young man had on his face. As supposed to the incident that occurred when Christian accidently pulls off the real killer's mask. Which is where Danny Burton thought they discover who he was? When in fact it was all her doing? When the opportunity presented itself when that incident occurs when Christian pulls off Danny's mask by accident. Which was the opening she needed to plan her next move. Which is to give Jason's cellphone to someone else that being the young man with the Michael Myers mask. That she confiscated while chasing Jason through the House of Horrors. Which he so happened to drop which was in her possession for the time being. Until she decided to get rid of it. By passing it along to the young man who they trace Jason's phone to. Which is where the whole mix up occurred between the two parties about the two separate incidents involving the mask being pull off. Which is how she exposed the two of them with the help of O'Malley? However, she still blames him for the murder of her brother Eric. That if he would have said something earlier to her about it, none of this wouldn't have occur. Then just like that Rochelle pull the trigger killing Grady O'Malley with one shot to the head. That all remains is Jill, Jason & Eli James who she has major plans for. As Rochelle ask Jill do, she understands now what she met by the bucket list she must beware of. Considering that it will result in death for her & her friends. That so far Rochelle manages to get even with the people that had something to do with her brother's death. However, Rochelle wanted Jill to suffer for what she done to Eric by returning a favor by killing one of her friends. Which was none other than Christian who because of her seal his fate. Who also played a part in her plan to get revenge on Danny Burton & Edgerrin James? Considering that she was the one who free Christian from his restraints. Who also place a walkie talkie by him so that he could hear everything that was going on between them & the killers? Which is how he knew everything that was going on that night at the House of Horrors. That it was because of her that Christian manages to save them both from certain death. Along with everyone else who face certain danger that night in the House of Horrors. Which seems to be the case as of now. That people are made to suffer the consequences due to her actions. Including the cast & crew of this film who die by her hands. That just like the original killers she is planning to get away with it. Although, she would have to make a few adjustments on how it all traces back to Eli James. As being the prime suspect in these killing of retribution of the killing of his father. Which wouldn't be that difficult to do. When everything that has happened all traces back to him. Considering that there is proof that he is the one responsible for the resurrection of the faces of death murder trial. That Rochelle has all sorts of evidence that leads to him being the killer. One being the gun he was carrying around with his fingerprints on it. That killed Timothy Jones also the knife she planned on him to make it seems convincing to police that it was all him. That in the end he allegedly committed suicide with the very gun he was carrying around, now that he avenges his father death. While she slips through the back door unnoticed without any hassle from anyone. Which is the story that is going to make headlines across the nation. As Rochelle told Jill that there will be only one survivor who make it through. That is going to give the details about what happened. That person being none other than Lisa who is the only one who doesn't know who she is?

Which is perfect considering that she isn't going to cause any trouble. That the slate will be clean with no evidence of her any where's around considering that she is now a ghost in the eyes of the public. That for all she knows Rochelle Mitchell is dead according to records.

CHAPTER 20

The End of an Era

That there will be no looking back once everything is finalize within putting things into perspective. As of finally putting an end to the Faces of Death conspiracy once & for all. That life will come to a full circle once the police realize how the missing links in the chain of events to the story all connects in the end. That Lisa will play an important role in how this story ends. That according to her story Eli James was the killer who murder everyone on set. Including Jill, Christian & Jason for that matter who wanted payback for his father. Who then committed suicide in the end considering that there was nothing else to live for? As Rochelle couldn't have written a better script than this one to ride off into the sunset undetected. That she will be willing to go on with the rest of her life as if nothing happened. Which seems like the perfect ending to a story that ends with the killer getting away with murder. As Rochelle reminded Jill ahead of time in the text message she sent after the conclusion of last year's event. That this is where things get interesting? In which she didn't disappoint how interesting things would get in the end. Considering the circumstances that had the dealing of being a part of the film's famous scene called Whodunnit? Which was a page Rochelle has taken from the film to turn a harmless game into a real-life scenario. By using all six of the Carson family attire to cause confusion within the cast & crew about who is the killer amongst them. That in the end they all paid the price. However, there was one thing Jill couldn't understand is how Rochelle manage to sound like the victims she has killed. Rochelle told her that she has a device that allows her to record the voices of others on set including her & her friends Jason & Christian. Which is the device she uses time & time again to lure them into a bad situation.

Which is how she was able to keep things interesting by disguising her voice with having the privilege of sounding like someone else. Which all ends with the killer's voice that she also recorded on the device. That voice being Eli James as the killer. Now all the while Rochelle was explaining everything to them it allows Jill the time, she needed to free her hands. That all Jill was waiting on is the right moment to catch Rochelle off guard. Considering that she would have to wait until the opportunity to present itself. Knowing that she doesn't stand a chance with the gun Rochelle has in her possession. Meanwhile Rochelle was preparing to get everything in place to killed Jason first by using a knife she pulled from the interior of the Ella Carson costume she had on. Since he is still dearly close to her heart. That Jill must sit & watch her beloved boyfriend be slaughter the way she slaughters Eric Johnson. Rochelle's only family she had left which was a promise she made to her mother that if anything happens to her. Then she would be responsible for her little brother. Considering that she got the two people responsible for her & Eric's mother's death. Which Jill tries to explain to her that it was Danny & Edgerrin James who were the ones who killed their mother & had her brother killed in the process. However, Rochelle disagrees with her statement & told her that she has already killed the two people behind her mother's murder. However, it was her who killed her brother & not Danny Burton or Edgerrin James for that fact. That she took the one thing that met something to her, that now she must watch the people that met something to her die in vain. However, just as Rochelle was getting ready to killed Jason. Jill yell to Lisa to stop her. When Rochelle turns around to see if Lisa was behind her. Jill seen her chance to seize the moment by surprising Rochelle when she least expected. As Jill took the rope that held her hands together to try & strangle Rochelle by placing the rope around her neck when she was distracted. Although, there wasn't any sign of Lisa every where's to be found. It was just a distraction to stop Rochelle from killing Jason while she takes advantage of the opportunity that was given to her. It then became a war between the two of them as they fought over who would be in control. It became a struggle as the surprise attack causes Rochelle to lose control of the gun & the knife she had. As Rochelle held on to dear life to not let the rope slip through her fingers. Which will result in certain death if she loses her handle on the rope which is the only thing that separates the rope from her neck is her hands. Meanwhile, Jason tries his best to get free so that he can assist Jill. Who is losing her advantage over Rochelle who is determined to not let this opportunity slip by? Of having the pleasure to avenge her brother's killer by doing whatever it takes to settle the score. Things turn bad to worse for Jill as Rochelle manages to break free from the strangle hold Jill had on her. Which turn into a nasty fight between the two of them as they fought over who would get to either the gun or the knife first. As the fight spill into the hallway of the tower making this by far one epic battle to content with as of who will rise victoriously in the end. That one way or another this fight wasn't going to end on a good note. That both women are fighting for dominance to see who would be the one to avenge their loved one. As Jill was fighting on the behalf of Christian, while Rochelle fought over the loss of her brother Eric. It would seem as if Jill had everything under control. That is until Rochelle have gotten the upper hand by surprising Jill with another knife she has hidden in away in her costume. It seems as if Rochelle had gotten the better of Jill. Who was on top of her with the knife bearing down toward Jill's shoulder? Jill then begins to scream out in pain as the tip of the blade pierce her shoulder tearing through her flesh. As a smile grew on the face of Rochelle by asking Jill how it feels to know her time is up. As Rochelle reminded Jill of the time when she got her to admit that it felt good to finally nail the bastard. Referring to her brother Eric who Jill didn't think twice about killing. Who did it with a smile on her face according to what occur that day when Jill admits it to Rochelle in their dormitory? Which was before Jill discover he was innocent in which she tries to explain to Rochelle. Although Rochelle wasn't trying to hear any excuses Jill may have. Considering that she is only doing this to try & cover up what she has done. Just like Danny Burton & Edgerrin James tries to do. That she deserves to die along with her boyfriend Jason who doesn't deserve to live. Considering that he too is partially to blame for all of this. That why should he be the only one that lives when everyone else who took part in that incident with Elizabeth Burton has die except for him. Which includes her stepbrother Eric Johnson who also didn't deserve what happen to him. Which infuriated Rochelle even move as she push the knife down deep into Jill's shoulder every time, she thinks of the trouble Jill has cause. That it was nice getting payback for the two people behind the killing of her brother. However, it was even sweeter of having the pleasure to kill the person responsible for killing her brother. However, just before delivering the final blow. A shot rings out from the gun that hit Rochelle in the chest knocking her off Jill. It seems as if Eli James had come to her rescue by using the last bullet to end the nightmare. Jill never thought that she would be glad to see

Eli James. As she then thanks him for saving her life. As she went over to check on Jason to assist him in getting himself free from the restraints, he had a hard time getting out of. Meanwhile Eli went over to see if Rochelle was dead. However, when he bent down to check her pulse, he felt a sharp object tear through his torso. As he was stab in his side by Rochelle who play possum by having him think that she was dead. Come to find out that she had on a protective vest under the costume. Which protected her from the bullet that he fired. She immediately pushes him aside & went after Jill to end this thing once & for all. However, Jason seen Rochelle coming & alerted Jill that she is still alive. Jill then begins to run as Rochelle was in hot pursuit. Jill then falls near the other knife that had falling in the struggle they had early on. As Rochelle again got on top of her to deliver the final blow as Rochelle ask Jill does, she has any final words before she dies. Jill then smiles & told her yes. As Jill then grabs the knife & stabs Rochelle in the neck & told her that she is sorry for killing her brother. Although she is also sorry for killing her in the process of having to kill them both due to a misunderstanding. Which is where the story ends for Rochelle as she dies instantly from the blow, she suffers of being stab in the neck. Considering that it was the only place where she wasn't protected by the vest. Where Jill could make an instant kill without having her suffer in pain that it would be quick & easy. As Jill still had a soft spot for her former friend considering that she old her that much for killing her brother. That there wasn't any animosity she felt toward her as Jill still consider Rochelle as her friend. That things could have been different between the two of them. If she would have just explained the situation to Jill about what she was going through. Then Rochelle would have seen that she met her no harm in thinking that she took pleasure in killing her brother. That it was just a misunderstanding that she wishes she could take back. That there is not a day she thinks about how it affects her as well. Which ended up with Jill crying her eyes out about what just transpired between her & Rochelle her best friend. As Jason went over to console her & to let her know that this is not her fault. As he told her to look at it from a different point of view that Rochelle is now join with her family.

CHAPTER 21

A New Lease on Life

As Jason told Jill that the nightmare is all over that they can go on with their lives that finally they can live in peace. Although it wouldn't be the same without their dear friend Christian. Whose life will be celebrated from years on end. Meanwhile in the hallway Jill & Jason heard Eli James cry out for help. As he seems to be in bad shape from the injury he suffered. As Jason attended to Eli wounds while Jill called the police. Eli told Jill to forget about calling the police because he has already called them. Jill couldn't thank Eli enough for saving her life. Although there was one thing, she wanted to know is at what point did he regain conscious to know what was going on. Eli told her that all the commotion between the two of them woke him up. Plus, he got some info from Jason who gave him a brief summary of the details. He needed to inform the police about what is going on. While the two of them were fighting. Which makes sense even though there were a few questions that needed to be answered. As Eli went ahead to answer the question for them. Considering that he already knew what they wanted to ask him. Like why he changed his name from Eli James to Elliot Smith. It was as simple, since he didn't want to be associated with a killer. As he didn't want any parts of the dealing that has to relate to his father Edgerrin James. Considering that Eli & his father Edgerrin James didn't have a close relationship to begin with. As he made it clear that there wasn't any animosity toward them for killing his father. That what his father did was inexcusable & that he didn't want any parts of it. Which is the reason why he changed his name although he did apologize to Jason for knocking him unconscious with the gun. Considering that he needed to by time to see who was the one trying to set him up. That he knew someone have gotten a *hold to his record & decided to share them with them. To make it seems as if he was the one behind the killings. In which case his intuition was right all along has he figure it to be someone they knew. Who wanted revenge for their loved one? However, he didn't expect it to be the stepsister of Eric Johnson. Which is safe to say that they all were surprised how things unfolded. That all because he had threatened Jill with the gun for her to hand over the cellphone. So, that she doesn't call the police on him. As he made it clear to Jill that he wasn't going to shoot her despite that he knew the killer would intervene. By not letting the cat out of the bag. As he purposely allows the killer to knock him out allegedly. For him find out who was it that was trying to frame him. As it turns out that his plan workout perfectly as Rochelle wasn't aware that he's been listening the whole time. When she thought that he was out for the count. As he sort of played possum for a while, until it was time to make a move. That he was about to make a move when Rochelle was about to killed Jason, but Jill intervenes as she manages to get loose from her restraints. As Jill & Jason was impress by how smart Eli was. As he jokingly told them that it runs in the family. As Jill & Jason couldn't help but to laugh at the pun intended to make fun of his dysfunctional family. However, the laugher would soon come to an end when they heard a voice asking them what's so funny. As it turns out that someone was Lisa who seems to be in good spirits. Even though, she had no idea what happened? So, Jill decided to give her the full story about who Rochelle was & how it all connects with the Faces of Death murderers Danny Burton & Edgerrin James. Not long afterward came the police with the paramedics to assist with the injured. As Jill gave her statement about what happened to the police who wanted a report on what all went on within the filming of this movie. While Lisa reported it to her team so that they could broadcasted it live across the country. It was made clear that there were no other survivors who made it through. Considering all the body bags that was being carry out of the tower. Although there was one individual who seem to have survive the assault from the killer. That person being none other than Christian who manage to survive all of what he's been through. Which was a miracle of how he was able to make it through considering how bad off he was. Which goes to show them how unpredictable life can be. Which is unbelievable as they all thought that he was dead. Which brought Jill & Lisa to tears as they couldn't believe it. As it was all smiles for Jason who spirits begin to lift with hope that his friend is going to be alright. As they all got into the ambulance with Christian to see to it that he makes it to the hospital without any complications. When they arrive at the hospital, they immediately rush Christian to surgery in order to save his life. Meanwhile, Jill, Jason & Lisa waited for the results from the doctors on the condition of their friend. Fast forward to one month later it seems as if Christian was doing fine with the help of his friends who help him with his rehabilitation. As it turns out that while Christian was in rehabilitation, he & Lisa manage to finish their book about the Faces of Death murders. Which would go on to sell millions in its first week of going live. As there were all sorts of interviews lining up for the four of them to be guest cohost on different shows. To talk about the book & how has it affect them in the long run. As the money begins to pour in as the book becomes a best seller in the New York's Times. Which puts the four of them in the spotlight for success as Christian became the co-founder of his own newspaper company. While Lisa became his personal reporter who deliver the goods to his newspapers. While Jill & Jason settle down in the country away from all the craziness of being famous. Although it seems as if they get recognize wherever they go. As being the it couple who survive the madness together. Even though the four of them took on a new role in their lives. They still manage to make time for one another to see each other occasionally. Meanwhile, there was an upcoming actor who made headlines by his outstanding performance by playing his father in the Faces of Death movie called Death of a Nightmare. A person none other than Eli James who seen the impact his last name has on the industry & decided to embrace the name for the time being. Although he didn't want his father's name to define who he is as a person. As that part of him is non-factor in how he was raise by his mother. It would seem as if they all have got a new lease on life as of how they manage to look toward to the future & not let the past define who they are as people. Looking to move on with their lives & continue to bring awareness to the victims who have suffer greatly in the turmoil. That time will only tell if people truly understand what the four of them went through for peace to be restore. Of how many lives that has been affect by all this chaos. That has occurred within these past couple of years. That all though they can't change what has happened. They still can shed some light on the cause that played a huge factor in their lives. As they all look back & wonder was it all worth the trouble that has affected so many lives in the process. Which ended up bad for them all who dares to underestimate the four of them thinking that they can get over. However, their focus as of now is what happens next in their journey to restore peace within the country. Hoping that the nightmare is indeed over for now as they all could rest easy. That was written in Jill's journal as a reminder that it is safe to say that she can truly move on with her daily life with her friends by her side.*

The End

Printed in the United States
by Baker & Taylor Publisher Services